INVINCIBLE VINCE

by
Joanne Thompson

AULTBEA
PUBLISHING LTD

Copyright details

Invincible Vince

First published in Great Britain by
Aultbea Publishing Company in 2005,
28 Church Street, Inverness IV1 1HB

Second Edition

ISBN 1905517017

Printed by Highland Printers Limited
Henderson Road, Inverness IV1 1SP

For Findlay and Daisy

What's All This About?

Hey you! Are you listening?

Yes you!

Can you keep a secret?

Good.

It's about Vince.

That's right, Vince. Him over there, playing in the garden.

He looks as ordinary as you or me, doesn't he? Living in a house just like you or me. Going to school just like you or me.

But actually, he's a little bit special.

You see, he's a *FYX/it*.

A *what* ?! I hear you cry!

A *FYX/it*.

FYX/it 27, to be precise.

Let me explain (and remember, this is top secret).

FYX/its are very rare people who live in our world, but every now and again have to carry out missions in Oops.

Oops?

Yeah, it's a bit like here, but more like there. And the Sess-Pitts have just moved in.

Sess-Pitts??

Yeah, they're the new family in town, and well, they're not very nice. They're like …like those awful neighbours who won't throw your ball back when it goes into their garden.

Or your friends' parents who make you tidy up when you've been to their house for tea.

Or grown ups who are always shouting and never listening.

And who always ask you to run errands for them.

And – well, you get the picture. They're all your worst people rolled into one.

And (and this is the nasty bit) if they don't like you. If, after ordering you around, they don't like all that you've done for them, they Pitt you.

They what??

Pitt you.

Squash you in a box.

A glass box.

So everyone can see.

Yes indeedy.

And only a *FYX/it* can get you out.

Nasty, hmmm?

Hey!

No need to worry!

You're not in Oops!

But look, there has been some pitting going on there today, and *FYX/it 27* does need to get into action. FAST.

Oh, but he can't! He doesn't actually *know* he's a *FYX/it* yet!

He's about to find out!!

1   The Adventure Begins

PLOP!

DAAAAH!

The wind had blown something out of a tree into Vince's bucket.

PWWW!

Water had splashed up Vince's nose and all over his snap cards.

His cousin Max Thwacks (that wasn't his real name) looked up from his cheating.

"HA! Wasat?"

"Nothing," muttered Vince hurriedly. He was desperate to have a look in the bucket, but he didn't want Max Thwacks to see. Max Thwacks had a habit of taking things away from Vince without asking. Vince would check it out later.

"My go," he said, but his Mum had appeared at the back door and picked up his baby sister Poppet, who was chewing on some mud.

"Tea!" yelled Mum.

Max Thwacks dropped his cards in a heap and thudded off inside, his big, clumsy feet tripping over a plant pot as he went.

Vince peered into the bucket to see what had plopped, but the water was too muddy.

Quick! He whisked out the whatever-it-was, stuffed it into his trouser pocket, and scooted down the garden for tea.

He wished he hadn't.

What a disaster!

Mum was panicking. She'd lost her "Italian Recipe Book" (whatever that meant), so her "*Ma-ca-roni cheese*" had turned out wrong…quite wrong.

EEER!

Vince wretched as he tried to scrape the globby white gunk away so he could eat his pasta, a process which a) failed, and b) took so long that he lost the dinner race with Max Thwacks.

GRRRR!!

Max Thwacks had wolfed his down so greedily that his disgusting mass of curly hair had disappeared into his plate.

SWODGE.

When he finally had to look up because there was no more food left, his hair had flicked the disgusting sauce all over Vince.

FLICK!

R-E-T-C-H-!

Dad had come in looking quite ridiculous. His t-shirt was wet with sweat from the gym and he was wearing flip flops with socks! SOCKS?!

FLIP. FLIP.

He'd taken one look at Mum's food and sighed, shaking his head. "You need to add this…bla" he'd said to Mum. "And that...bla. And anyway, you don't need a recipe, you go by the taste...bla."

Mum didn't speak for the rest of tea.

You'd think it couldn't get much worse.

Well, you haven't met Max's Mum – Jelly Melly (that's not her real name either). She turned up just before pudding.

BOO.

She was as thin as the thinnest twig on the tree.

EEER.

She smelt of sprouts.

EEEEEEEEER.

And she talked non-stop through slimy, fire engine-red lips (Triple EEEER):

"Wellthecleanerdidn'tturnupsoIhadtomopthekitchenfloorcanyouI MAGINE!AndthenthemicrowavebrokesoIhadtousetheovenTHEO VEN!AndthenthechildminderhadaheadachebutImanagedtobookM axieintoafterschoolclubandthenhehaddinnerclubandbedtimecluban dnextweekhe'sinswitchcluballweekthankgoodnesssoImightfinally getachancetoreadChow!…BLA…BLA…Andthenhesaidwhatpeac ock???…HAHAHAHA!"

YAWN.

She was so boring Vince nearly fell asleep in his plate of slop.

She refused to eat Mum's food, but still managed to shovel in SIXTEEN mouthfuls of jelly (Vince counted), and give the rest to "darling Maxie", so there was none left for Vince!

None!

That was it!! Vince was going to starve!!!!

When oh when were they going to leave???

Well, not before they had played hopscotch and Max Thwacks had pushed Vince over, and called him "Puny Bottom!" (Vince called Max "Stinky Bottom" back, which he was quite pleased with!).

And not before Max had snatched the packet of chocolate fudge fingers and scoffed the lot (Vince had snatched the rest of Max's

6

apple in return, which he realised wasn't a complete victory, but it did make him feel better).

And not before Max had bounced so hard on Vince's space hopper on purpose that it had burst (Vince could only vow that revenge would be total).

To top it all, Jelly Melly had slapped a great big slurpy goodbye kiss on Vince's cheek when he wasn't looking.

Nooo!

Vince had wiped his face, scowling.

Still, at least they were leaving.

And, as they opened the front door, Vince grinned.

He'd remembered the Thing in his pocket.

Perhaps the day wouldn't be all bad after all!

He began racing up the stairs, shouting a quick "Bye!" without looking back.

He charged into his room, shut the door tight, and waited a second to check no one had followed him up. With a trembling hand, he pulled the Thing out of his pocket.

DAAAAH!

He threw it on the floor in front of him as if it were on fire!

It was PINK!!!

For once he'd managed to keep something from Max Thwacks...and now it was PINK!

Vince kicked it under his bed in disgust and went off to get ready for bed.

2   Sweets!!!

SIGH. TOSS. TURN.

Snooze?

No.

TOSS. TURN. SIGH.

It was a couple of hours later, and Vince couldn't sleep.

What a rubbish day he'd had.

Perhaps if he sighed a bit louder, Dad might hear him and stop playing chess on the computer and come and give him a rugby tackle.

SIGH…

SPLAT!

What was that?

Vince sat up in bed.

He blinked into the darkness, holding his breath.

Nothing.

He lay back down cautiously and blinked a bit more quickly.

SPLAT! SPLAT!

There it was again.

He jumped out of bed and turned on his light.

And jumped away from the switch.

Daaah!

There was something new on his wall.

Several new things, in fact.

He peered more closely, keeping his distance in case they were spiders.

No, they were…letters.

He moved closer.

Three pink (he sighed) letters.

"G-A-R" he read slowly, and screwed up his nose. "Gar? Gar? Sounds pretty babyish and pink to me" he muttered scornfully.

SPLAT!

OW!

Another one had appeared and landed right on his ear! At once it started sizzling like a sausage in a pan! It was burning his skin!

He fell to the floor to wrestle it off.

Ooh, it was hot. Oooh, it was …squidgy. He couldn't get it off his fingers. He was panicking now, writhing around the floor. He might have to call Dad.

But wait a minute.

The burning had stopped and…what was that smell?

It certainly wasn't sausages.

Something rather lovely and sweet was wafting up from his fingers.

Could it be…?

He licked the letter.

Yes!

Oh what a lovely…pink…taste! It was some kind of jellied sweet!

And it seemed to have come from under his bed.

Suddenly, the Pink Thing wasn't seeming so rubbish after all!

As he chewed, he began to crawl towards his bed.

But…SPLAT! The Thing was firing again.

Vince retreated and turned to look at the wall.

SPLAT! SPLAT!

He blinked for a moment, making sure he'd got the letters right.

"GARDEN" he read.

He raised his eyebrows, thinking.

"Err…yes," he said, finally, nodding his head. "I did find you in the garden."

And then he stopped, realising he wasn't quite sure who he was speaking to.

He waited.

And then sure enough, SPLAT! SPLAT! SPLAT! SPLAT!!!!

The Thing was going mad. Perhaps it was cross! Had he said the wrong thing?

No, wait, it had stopped.

There was a new word on the wall.

He began to spell.

"A-D-V-E-N…"

This wasn't looking like a word he knew.

He shook his head and had some more sweet instead.

There was a long pause.

Vince looked nervously under the bed.

And then – SPLAT! SPLAT! SPLAT!

Just three more.

"F-U-N"

Vince nodded excitedly.

"Ooh, yes," he said politely, "we do have fun in the garden."

He smiled a hopeful smile in the direction of the bed.

Two more letters came whizzing out immediately.

Vince ducked out of the way.

"G-O" he read.

And then gasped.

Very slowly, he turned to the bed.

"You want me to go in the garden…now?" he said weakly.

He knew what was coming.

SPLAT! SPLAT! SPLAT!

He didn't need to look at the three letters.

3   Into the Garden

Vince thought quickly.

"Actually it's dark now," he croaked. "Er…we'll have more fun tomorrow."

He smiled weakly at the bed again.

Nothing.

Vince breathed a sigh of relief. It seemed that that was OK with the Pink Thing.

Maybe he'd got time for one more jelly before he went to sleep.

He reached out towards the wall.

But suddenly – WHIZZ! WHIZZ! WHIZZ!

The letters began shooting off the wall and back under the bed.

"No!" cried Vince, trying to catch the letters as they flew. "No! Don't take the sweets away!"

WHIZZ! WHIZZ!

There were only a couple left.

"OK!" spluttered Vince. "OK! I'll go now! Straight away! Just leave me one sweet!!"

The whizzing stopped.

Vince licked his lips and grabbed the last sweet.

"Thank you," he whispered, putting the jelly in his mouth.

But it seemed there was no time to savour it.

For the flying jellies were back, whizzing out again from under the bed and forming a line behind him.

As he looked frantically over his shoulder, they began to push him towards the door.

"Wait!" yelped Vince as he shunted forward. "I need to take some things!!"

He shot to his secret stash between the wall and the bed. After a quick scramble, he found his torch.

FLICK. FLICK.

Daaaah!

It wasn't working! It needed new batteries!

Vince looked wildly around.

AHA! He opened one of his drawers and pulled out his glow-in-the-dark helicopter pyjamas! These should help him see alright!

"Ready!" he shouted, putting them on, and grabbing one of his bendy swords, in case he needed to charge through any spider's webs on the way.

"Oops sorry!" he muttered as he trod on several jellies which were now covering his whole floor. "Now, hang on, we've got to get past Dad."

Vince crept along the landing towards the study door.

They were in luck!

Dad had his radio on full blast and was engrossed in his chess game.

Vince and his jelly friends slipped silently past and were downstairs in a flash.

"Wait!" whispered Vince. Eagle-eyed Mum may not be so easy.

But luck was smiling on them again. She was hoovering the den (she loved cleaning – well so it seemed to Vince). Anyway, she would never hear them!

Vince raced through the kitchen, flung the back door open, and…stopped.

Oh.

It was much quieter then he thought.

And – oh, much darker than he thought.

He looked down at his helicopter top.

Hmmm.

Not much light coming from there.

Vince blinked into the night.

Seems the jellies weren't bothered about the dark.

They had whizzed past him and disappeared towards the back of the garden.

"But…"

Vince swallowed hard.

He stepped out and began to follow them.

PANT. PANT.

All he could hear was the sound of his own breathing.

PANT. PANT. PANT.

It was getting faster and faster.

Daaah!

He waved his sword as tiny creatures flew into his face. Shadows moved scarily along the walls.

PANT. PANT. PANT. PANT.

The wind began rustling the leaves of the trees. He quickened his step.

PANT. PANT. PANT. PANT. TICK.TICK.TICK.TICK!!!!!!

What was that?

TICK.TICK.TICK.TICK!!!!!!

AAAAGH!

Hundreds and hundreds of twigs were falling on his head!

TICK.TICK.TICK.TICK!!!!!!

Down his neck! Down his legs!!

TICK.TICK.TICK.TICK!!!!!

They sounded like thunder in the silence of the garden.

"Aaaaagh!"

 Vince had to stop walking.

He jigged up and down on the spot, trying to dodge the twigs.

And then suddenly, something hard and prickly grabbed him around his waist and swung him high into the air.

4 Talking Trees and Silly Games

"WAAAAH!" cried Vince.

"Gotcha!" cried a voice.

What?

Vince was thrust against the wall – DOOF! – and pinned there by something bendy and wirey.

"AAAAGH!"

Leaves and twigs began scratching at him from all sides.

"OOOWWWW!"

It was like being attacked by a million hairbrushes all at once.

And now something was fluttering in his ear.

"What you up to, hey?" whispered the voice, as Vince wriggled and kicked. "No one comes out here at night unless they're invited, and I don't see your invitation anywhere!"

"The pink jellies brought me!" screamed Vince, and immediately wished he hadn't.

"Ah," mocked the voice, shaking Vince harder. "Did the pretty dinkums jellies taste nice goo goo ga ga…?"

"Daaaah!" Vince kicked more furiously, cross with himself for letting on about the Pink Things.

"Watch out!" came another voice. "You're letting him get away! Give him to me!"

Vince was yanked from his wirey trap and pulled across the bricks of the wall.

"H-e-l-p!" he yelled. "O-U-CH!"

He'd been perched on top of something rough and spikey which was digging into his bottom.

Voices were debating around him.

"What d'you reckon, Scritch? In the dustbin?"

"Yeah, nice one Scratch, best place for him."

"Let ME dump him in, I'm closest!"

Who was that?

Now Vince was suddenly tugged from below!

"NOOOO!"

"Get lost Shorty, he's ours!"

Vince was pulled up again.

"Give him HERE!"

Down Vince went.

"OWWWW!" he yelled. His body was stretched so much he thought it might burst.

"Somebody help me…!"

"BOYS!!! STOP THAT IMMEDIATELY!"

Oooh – somebody WAS helping him!!!

The tugging stopped for a moment.

"But Boss, it's an intruder!" shouted a voice.

"Yeah! We need to get rid of him," came another.

"IT'S VINCE, YOU TWIGIOTS!" thundered Vince's saviour. "We've been waiting for him all day! Let him GO!"

There was the sound of huffing and hawing, and then Vince was tipped unceremoniously onto the ground.

"OW!"

Silence.

He rubbed his bottom and blinked nervously into the darkness.

Something was glinting by the garden gate.

He screwed up his eyes.

And shook his head.

That couldn't be right.

He thought there was a pair of sunglasses in the tree in the wall.

"Are you OK Vince?"

Vince jumped back in shock.

Now there was a mouth in the tree as well! Just below the sunglasses.

He swallowed hard.

"OK?"

The mouth had opened again.

Vince blinked for a moment, and then nodded very, very slightly.

"Good. I'm Polly Smart. Don't worry about the Boys, they're just doing their job."

Vince looked round. Now he could make out the trees which had attacked him: the rose, the honeysuckle, the holly. They were ALL wearing sunglasses, and eyeing him suspiciously.

Vince swallowed and turned back to the tree by the gate.

"What… job?" he frowned, looking down at his hand which seemed to be bleeding a bit.

The tree leant in.

"We're looking for *FYX/its*," she whispered again, and winked.

Vince screwed up his nose.

"You've been in my *FYX/it* file for a while Vince. Now the perfect job's come up for you. I need you to help me remove a Family from Oops."

Oops?

Polly read Vince's face.

"It's a place sort of like here, but different," she explained.

Badly, thought Vince.

But Polly clearly didn't have time for anything better.

"This Family," she continued quickly. "They're called the Sess-Pitts, and they're disgusting. They're lazy, selfish, grubby aristocrats, with a nasty habit of squashing people they don't like into glass boxes and putting them on display."

Vince blinked at her.

"ALIVE," Polly added, for good measure, ignoring the change in Vince's face.

She continued.

"It's a practice other aristocratic families have tried to copy over the centuries, and it's become known as 'Pitting'. It's highly illegal of course. We don't always get to hear about it, but I know from other *FYX/its* that there's some going on right now."

Vince gave a weak smile. Actually, he didn't much like the sound of Oops.

And he'd suddenly realised that he was talking to a tree, and he wasn't sure he should be doing that.

But Polly was leaning in even closer, and whispering heavily, and slowly: "Come on, Vince. We need you. Only *FYX/its* can outpitt the Pitts. Are you up to the challenge?" She was speaking more quickly now. "Are you *FYX/it 27,* Invincible Vince? Or a No-More-Sweets-And-Scrubbed-out-of-my-File Piddly Prince???"

Vince stared at her gravely for a moment.

And then burst out laughing.

"Piddly Prince! HA!"

He rolled onto his back, giggling insanely.

Then he stopped.

He was no Piddly Prince!

He was also rather fond of Polly's sweets.

He jumped to his feet.

"*FYX/it…*" he struggled to remember the number. "*FYX/it fer fer*" he mumbled, nodding at Polly Smart hopefully. "In…visible

Vince ready for action…er… POLLY!"

He shouted the last bit to make up for the first bit.

"What do I have to do?!"

"I knew you wouldn't let me down," nodded Polly, her branches bristling over the gate. "Come and stand next to me on this loose paving stone."

Vince stepped forward.

"OK," said Polly, leaning in closer than ever. "You've got to do the Oops Jump to get into Oops, but it's a secret."

She looked up towards the other trees in the garden, who were now busying themselves trying to flick one of Vince's footballs between them.

"Hey!" Vince moved to stop them, but the tree caught him with one of her long trailing branches.

"Aaaagh!" Vince gave a terrified yelp. Not again!

"Come on Vince, you need to focus on another game now."

Vince was shaking, but he could never resist a game: "W-What g-game?" he stuttered.

Polly raised her eyebrows.

"You know that game where you jump and have to NOT tread on the lines?"

Vince nodded; he was fantastic at that game.

"Well," said Polly very quickly and very quietly, "you'll have to tread ON the lines and fall over a lot."

She pulled away from Vince and started whistling casually.

5   Time for the Oops Jump

Vince was aghast.

Tread ON the lines?!

Fall over ON PURPOSE?! (which he had to admit was fun, but he couldn't let anyone see him do that in a game situation).

He shook his head.

But Polly was ready for him.

"Listen Vince, we don't have much time," she whispered. "I know you're very good at the game. But this is an even trickier one, because, well, look, the lines are much thinner than the spaces, aren't they? I'll bet you CAN'T jump on the lines around this slab."

At these words, Vince leapt into the air and came crashing down on a line.

"Aaaargh!" His bottom took a bashing.

"Good," said Polly, taking a nervous look out into the garden. "Now the Oops Jump goes like this." She whispered a rhyme in Vince's ear:

> "Check behind! Check in front!
> It's got to be all clear when you do the Oops Jump!
> Run round the line as fast as you can,
> Now race backwards to where you began.
> Fling your arms and rock your head
> Blow a loud raspberry and lift your leg.
> Wibble and wobble like you don't care,
> And JUMP! When you land, you should be there!"

"Ooops! JUMP! Ooops! JUMP! OOOOOOOPS!" yelled Vince.

He huffed loudly and flung his arms by his side. "I can't remember all that!" (except the bit about blowing raspberries, he thought, obviously).

"You'll be surprised," whispered Polly. "Just make sure you head for the line when you jump. Now, take some more of these with you, they may come in useful."

She thrust one of her branches towards Vince. A handful of the pink jellied sweets were sitting on a leaf on the end of it.

Oh no, no. Vince stepped back, shaking his head. There was no way he was going to touch those things which had burnt and embarrassed him so badly.

Polly's leaves were rustling. "Come on *FYX/it 27*," she hissed. "You must be properly armed."

Vince sniggered. Armed? With a load of pink sugary stuff! Ha!

Hang on a minute...Armed?????

ARMED????

Oops was sounding less appealing again.

Maybe he could just...

Too late! At a flick of Polly's branch, the jellied sweets jumped from the leaf and disappeared into his trouser pocket.

No!

Vince slapped his hands over the pocket, but the opening had disappeared.

Huh???

He looked wildly at Polly Smart, but she had moved on, speaking more quickly than ever.

"Good. Now, I've also arranged for a team to help you out when you arrive."

Ooh. Vince's eyes grew wide. That didn't sound so bad! He LOVED being in charge!

"I'll be back here with the Boys, covering you from behind," continued Polly, "making sure no one follows you in. We had to stop your blundering cousin getting too close earlier."

Aaaaah.

Vince blinked for a moment.

Max HAD tripped over a plant pot, which Vince didn't remember ever being there before.

He swallowed.

These trees were clever.

Could he really trust them?

Was he really sure he wanted to do this?

But wait…his legs had started twitching of their own accord. There was no going back.

Think.

Think.

He began to chant the rhyme, jumping down, jumping up, scooting and wiggling like mad.

"Ooops! Ooops! OOOOOOOPS!"

BUMP. OWWW!

Nothing.

Just a sore bottom.

He tried again.

"Oops!!" BUMP.

Nothing.

"It's not WORKING! It's just hurting and making my trousers fall down!" he shouted.

Polly didn't answer.

Vince hoiked up his trousers.

OK. One more time for luck.

"Ooops! Ooops! OOOOOOOPS!"

He leapt as high as he could. He screwed up his nose and gritted his teeth, waiting for the painful smack of the pavement.

But none came.

Instead, his feet were suddenly whisked above his head. His legs felt as tall as chimneys and he realised they had stretched over the wall!

WEEEEEEE!

His face spread into a very wide grin.

The adventure had begun.

6   Vince Lands in Oops

WEEEEE!

Vince liked Oops!

He was sliding down the longest slide he had ever slid down.

WEEEEEEE!

The longer he slid, the faster he went!

WEEEEEEE!

His hair was standing on end!

OOOH!

A wind was rushing past his ears.

WOOOO!

His face was stretched backwards into a silly grin.

EEEEEEE!

His eyes were wide open like a startled rabbit.

BLINK. BLINK. BLINK.

Errrr…

Actually, they were a bit dry now.

BLINK. BLINK.

This wasn't quite so much fun.

BLINK.

Alright. That was enough.

H-E-L-P!

BUMP! BOUNCE! BOING!

Oh.

He'd landed.

Or had he??

He'd stopped sliding, but he hadn't really stopped moving.

BOING! BOING!

He was bouncing around on his bottom like he was in some sort of bouncy castle.

Fantastic!

He bounced onto his feet and whooped around a bit.

Maybe he could even scrabble back up the slide for another go!

BOING!

THUD!

OW!

Something hard had dropped onto his head.

He looked down at the floor.

It was a small green box.

BOING!

He bounced over to pick it up.

THUD!

OW!

Something else fell on his head!

Daaah!

He looked up.

Shelves.

Boxes.

Hundreds of coloured boxes.

All green.

And – Bounce – Daaah!

Every time he bounced, one fell off.

Vince blinked up at them for a moment.

And then he bounced again, looking very hard at the walls.

Wobble.

CATCH!

Vince was ready with his hand this time.

Just as he thought.

Bouncy castle walls!

Covered in boxes of…he picked one up.

And his eyes LIT up!

JELLY!

Wahoo!

He began jumping again, dodging the boxes this time.

Wahoo!

"Hey!"

BOING!

Vince bounced round.

Who said that!!?

He looked from side to side.

PING!

There. Over there.

There was a door.

It had just ping'd shut.

Someone was here!

He screwed up his nose.

Suddenly he began to wonder just what he was going to find in Oops.

Hmm.

Right, no more bouncing.

Cautiously, he slipped and slithered over the rubbery surface and reached out to the door.

PING!

It sprung back open at his touch.

Daaah!

Three faces wearing big red rubbery hats loomed before him in the doorway!

Vince jumped back and bounced onto his bottom.

THUD!

OW!

Daaah! Forgot the catch!

He rubbed his head and looked up.

If he hadn't been so scared, he would have laughed out loud at the sight before him.

The face on the left had a fringe of red hair so long that you couldn't see her eyes.

The one in the middle wore sunglasses as big as saucers so you couldn't see her eyes.

And the third had pulled her hat down way over her eyes.

All of a sudden the three of them made an "oo" shape with their lips and held their hands in front of them.

"Told you!!" boasted the fringy one, and the three of them turned and ran off.

Well, bounced off.

Vince sat blinking for a moment at the open doorway.

BUMPF…BUMPF…BUMPF

As he listened to the rhythmic bouncing on the other side, a thin snake of steam began drifting through.

And then suddenly –

CLATTER!

What was that?

"OCH!"

Who was that???

POO-EEEE!

Oh, he couldn't STAND that!!

A smell of rotten vegetables was wafting his way.

He put his fingers over his nose and blinked at the doorway.

He'd have to take a look.

Slithering as slowly as was possible, he made his way across and gingerly peeped over the rubbery doorstep.

His eyes grew very, very wide.

7 Check Out the Oops Kitchen!

It was a kitchen.

Quite the maddest kitchen Vince had ever seen.

It was hot.

It was steamy.

And it was moving all the time.

WOBBLE!

Just like the jelly cupboard. Everything was red and rubbery: the walls, the tables, the chairs.

WOBBLE.

The fridges, the freezers, the ovens.

WOBBLE.

The blenders, the juicers, the whisks. Even the plates stacked high and the spoons dangling low!

BOING. BOING.

And slipping, sliding, bouncing around it were zillions of chefs trying to cook.

BOING.

Tall.

Short.

Fat.

Thin.

SLIP.

Rubbery red hats. Red jackets. Red trousers.

Oh, and blue ones.

No – pink!

Sorry, green!

Derrrrr!

Vince stared at them, open mouthed, his head whizzing from side to side like he was watching a super speedy tennis match.

The chefs poured, they tossed, they boiled, they chopped. They grilled, they roasted, they fried, they toasted.

Stirred!

Cut!

Spilt!

Whisked! Mashed! Blitzed! Minced!

OOOF!!!

Vince rubbed his eyes.

It was too much!

He couldn't keep up.

"GRRRR!"

But wait.

One chef was easier to watch.

One chef wasn't racing.

One chef was prowling.

Like a lion through a pack of startled zebras.

Vince couldn't see much of him. Just a velvety golden hat. There weren't any others that colour.

And this chef really seemed to be floating around the kitchen.

Vince ducked down and squinted through the table legs to check his feet were actually touching the ground.

Oooh. It was busy down there again.

Blue trousers.

Blue socks (no shoes…?).

Green trousers.

More socks (no SHOES???).

Golden trousers.

Aha!

Slippers.

Slippers!!!?

Vince blinked very fast and clapped his hand to his mouth, desperate to laugh.

The golden chef was wearing the biggest, most ridiculous pair of slippers he had EVER seen!

Well, at least he thought they were slippers. They looked a bit like the comedy furry bears that Dad had bought Mum for Christmas to keep her feet super cosy.

They were pure white, and they puffed up over his feet like a whole bag of cotton wool buds bundled together.

HA!

He started to giggle as the slippers wafted around the rubbery floor like low-flying clouds.

But despite their RIDICULOUS appearance, Vince was impressed.

They were certainly stopping the chef from sliding around.

How DID they work…???

He was so engrossed that he didn't notice them change direction and come straight for him.

Suddenly a great roar filled the kitchen above his head.

"RAAAARRRR**@!****"

Vince looked up in terror.

Glaring down at the counter right in front of him was the most ferocious face Vince had ever seen.

He much preferred the slippers.

The face was rough. It was bristly. It was covered in scars. Its mane of golden hair was dripping wet.

It was chewing slowly on some food.

And it didn't like it.

"RAAAARRRR**@!****!" the chef spat the food out. "PINK CHEFS! This is Sweaty McCloud's kitchen! Not your local burger bar!!!! Throw these away and start again!!"

Chefs in pink hats bumped over to the counter. "Yes chef!" they mumbled and grabbed the pan.

GLUG...CLATTER... BUMPF...

"RAAAARRRR**@!****!" roared "Sweaty" as they jostled past.

Vince shrunk back. Sweaty wafted on his way, watching, listening, tasting and roaring.

"RAAAARRRR**@!****! Yellows! You bunch of flannel shoes! Paah! Call these Brussels sprouts? Give me texture! Give me taste!!"

"Yes Chef!"

PSSSSSH! BUMPF!

"Reds! Where's that jelly?" His eyebrows met above his nose as he frowned furiously at them. "You forgot????? How could you forget? What were you up to in that cupboard? Playing boil the bagpipes??"

The Reds were bouncing round him frantically, trying to tell him something.

"Grrr! Off! Get lost and get cooking!!!"

"Yes Chef!"

The Reds bounced away shaking their heads.

"Blues! STOP! STOP!"

The room fell silent for a moment. Everyone was staring at his shaking finger which was pointing at a counter where some chefs had been throwing food onto a plate .

"Our guests eat with their eyes as well as their mouths! Give me pretty food! OCH! Give me clean plates!"

There was a pause.

And then –

"Yes Chef!"

BUMPFCRASHPSSSSSSSSH!…the noise began again.

And Sweaty continued on his prowl, dripping more by the second.

He grabbed the tea towel which hung from his shoulder, and twirled it round into a long thin stick shape. He began flicking it at open cupboard doors, slamming them shut.

He flicked at plates on the edges of tables.

At chefs who were being too slow.

And then he stopped.

Vince craned to see what was happening.

He was looking at something on a surface of a counter.

Suddenly he opened out his tea towel and began rubbing furiously at it. When he had finished he held up his tea towel and shook it in disgust. Blobs of white gunk flew everywhere.

"NATTERLIE SESS-PITT!!!" he snarled.

The kitchen came to a standstill once more.

"YOU WILL RUIN MY KITCHEN!!!"

8   Vince Meets Sweaty McCloud

Sweaty was bent over the counter, beating it with his fists.

"I WILL NEVER BE RID OF YOU SESS-PITTS!!" he sobbed. "I …WILL …NEVER… GET…THREE" …sob, "STARS!!! Someone will beat me to it!"

There was a sympathetic sigh from the chefs around him. Some turned to look at a wall.

Vince followed their gaze.

There was a chart hanging next to the wobbly sink.

"Sweaty's Star Chart," read Vince in a whisper, and held his breath.

He LOVED star charts!

And look! This one was a race track!

Fantastic!

It was winding its wispy way across the page like a swirl of steam.

And there was Sweaty nearly at the end of the track, sitting in …Vince screwed up his nose…sitting in a super-huge floaty slipper car!

Ha!

Wearing a tin foil helmet!

Brilliant!

The car had two massive golden stars on the side of it.

And Sweaty was in a kind of pit stop called "Last Star Pick Up".

A team in silver boilersuits were holding a hose with a star on the end of it. They were trying to stick it on the car, but the hose wasn't quite long enough.

Vince craned to read the words under the pit stop: "3 Stars!! Congratulations! Your prize: A week in The Everclean Kitchen".

Vince screwed up his nose.

He wasn't sure about that prize. Personally, he was a fan of the "you choose your reward" variety of Star Chart. Last time, when he'd managed not to steal Poppet's favourite bunny and hide it somewhere even he couldn't remember, for a whole week, he'd chosen a Trouncer Tank! It was fantastic, with massive green…

Oooh.

Vince's daydream was brought to a sudden, unpleasant end.

"RAAAARRRR**@!****!"

Sweaty had stopped howling.

"RAAAARRRR**@!****!"

And started roaring at his gaping chefs.

"What are you all staring at??" The chefs looked away hurriedly. "Have you any idea what time it is!!?"

He looked in the direction of a row of ten lights which Vince hadn't noticed before. Three lights were lit red.

 "Three minutes to production!" yelled Sweaty. "Get cooking!"

The chaos began again, worse than ever, as the chefs rushed to be ready in time. They screeched round counters, bashing into the corners as they bounced.

BUMPF…CRASH!...AAAAAGH!...OUT OF MY
WAY…CLANG

"How long will I wait for my Brussels???" bellowed Sweaty.

"Thirty seconds, Chef," came the reply.

"RIGHT!! PLACES THEN!"

The chefs had begun collecting into groups of colour, like Vince
and his friends had to do on sports day. The chefs were huddled
together excitedly, jostling each other into position.

On Sweaty's command, one chef from each team took their place
at a huge slimy table that ran like a river through the kitchen. At
each place was a bowl the same colour as their clothes.

Hang on, there was a gap. There was one white bowl with no chef.
In fact, come to think of it, there were no white rubbery hats at all.

Vince frowned.

DINGALINGALING!

A thunderous bell rang out above the din of the machines and the
steam.

The first bowl in the line – the yellow one – lit up and began
jigging around.

"Brussels!" shouted the Yellow chef sitting at the table." One of
his fellow Yellows bounced up and tipped some horrible green
blobs into the bowl. The bowl jigged more ferociously.

"DON'T LET IT FALL!" barked Sweaty.

"Masher!" yelled the Yellow one, holding the bowl more tightly.

Another Yellow chef threw a masher towards him and the
mashing began.

Vince's head moved up and down as the whole scene bounced in front of his eyes.

What on earth were they going to make??

DINGALINGALING!

"Transfer! Transfer!" yelled Sweaty.

"Transfering!" the Yellow chef tipped the sludge from his bowl into the green bowl next to him, which had already started flashing and jigging.

"Reds! Get back to your stations!!" Sweaty roared with anger as the three chefs that had found Vince earlier started dragging him and pointing in Vince's direction.

Sweaty tried to kick them away with his huge shoes. "Get off! OFF! We'll miss the last bell, and…"

He stopped.

He'd seen Vince.

The whiskers on his chin bristled again as his mouth snarled into a sneer. He growled for a moment under his breath.

"Well, well, well," he muttered finally.

Vince tried to smile.

But Sweaty was on him in a flash.

"What time d'you call this, hey, you pair of flannel shoes?!"

If Vince hadn't been so scared, he would have said that was a bit rich, considering what Sweaty was wearing on his feet. Instead, he tried to look past the chef to the row of lights.

Sweaty blocked his way with his snarling face.

"What've you been doing? Playing hopscotch in the park??" he roared.

Vince wondered momentarily how Sweaty knew what he'd had been doing that morning, but the chef had already grabbed his jacket.

"Get into position!! You've got two minutes before we get to White. And get those boots off in my kitchen!"

He yanked Vince over the doorstep, threw him towards the table and padded off in disgust.

9   Cook? Me???

Vince could hardly breathe.

He blinked at the table in front of him.

What did Sweaty mean: "Get to White?"

He looked at the table. Did he want him to sit by the bowl??? But he didn't know what to do! He wasn't a chef!!

He reached up an arm to scratch his head, confused.

Scratch. Scratch. Scr…

Hang on…that didn't feel like his head.

Vince rolled his eyes slowly upwards.

Oh no.

Oh No!!!!

He wasn't!

He was!!!

He couldn't be!

He could!!!

He was wearing a white…rubbery…hat!!!

He looked back at the kitchen.

Then he looked slowly downwards…and groaned.

No more glow in the dark pyjamas. Just…black and white check trousers. Tight white jacket with lots of shiny buttons.

He WAS a White chef!!

But where was his team???

And anyway, he didn't know how to cook!

And…

Sweaty was shouting again.

"White chef, thirty seconds and counting!"

Vince jumped to attention, sending his white hat flying as he scrambled to his feet.

He grabbed the hat and bounced as quickly as he could to the rubbery red chair beside the white bowl.

He sat down and boing'd there uncertainly for a second.

The Red team next to him were going mad. The chef at the table seemed to be blasting whatever was in the red bowl with some kind of hot air machine, while his helpers were jumping up and down furiously behind him on some kind of pump which was providing the air.

Suddenly a huge alarm began to sound.

WEEEEE-WOOOO-WEEEE-WOOOO

His bowl began to jiggle madly in front of him. Before he could think, the gunk from the red bowl had been tipped into his white bowl.

WEEEEE-WOOOO-WEEEE-WOOOO

Vince jigged his knees up and down in despair. The alarm was getting louder, and Sweaty was getting sweatier.

"Get on with it!" he bellowed.

"Yes, but on with what?" thought Vince frantically, as his bowl began to flash and…wait a minute. Some words were appearing on the side. Help at last! What did it say…?? Vince read quickly.

ADD WOBBLE.

What???

Vince read it again to be sure.

ADD WOBBLE.

"But…But…" Vince's heart thumped as he looked desperately around for something wobble-like.

But he was too late.

WOOP WOOP WOOP

A new siren was sounding.

Sweaty slammed his fists onto a table in anger.

The other chefs began pleading with him to allow the dish to go without the wobble.

"No!" cried Sweaty. "No food leaves Sweaty McCloud's kitchen unless it is perfect! PERFECT!! We start again!"

10　Vince is in Deep Trouble

Uh oh.

Vince had a sneaky suspicion this might all be his fault.

The other chefs along the line were yelling and shaking their fists at him.

And Sweaty had disappeared in a rage.

Where was he…?

Ooh. He was here!

The dripping chef was beside Vince, ranting in his ear:

"Talking jibberish, cooking rubbish…just as bad as the last White chef, hey?! We've all missed the bell again because of you White idiots."

Vince leaned away as Sweaty's face got nearer and nearer.

"I don't know why we bother training you! All you've got to do is put the wobble in the jelly. Easiest job of all! And you mess it up every time!!"

Sweaty blinked fiercely at Vince for a moment. Then he stalked away in disgust, yelling as he went.

"I will not have shoddy chefs damaging the reputation of my kitchen!" The other chefs shook their heads. "Lipsticks! He's all yours! Take him to the tower to join his other silly White friend! The Sess-Pitts can take care of them both!"

"What?!" Vince looked wildly around.

The chefs around the kitchen started laughing and sneering and clapping their hands rhythmically.

"Lipsticks! Lipsticks! Lipsticks!" they chanted.

Vince still couldn't see anything.

"Lipsticks! Lipsticks –"

"Alright! Enough you lot!" roared Sweaty. "Back to your cooking! NOW!"

As the chefs slithered away, Vince was left alone at the table.

He waited.

Nothing.

His breathing quickened.

The suspense was killing him.

DING.

What was that?

He looked all around.

He couldn't see anything, but…

WHOOOO.

There was a cool draught coming from his right.

He looked to the wall.

Nothing.

He looked back at the table.

WHOOOO.

He rubbed his neck crossly.

Maybe there was a door left open.

WHOOOO.

He glanced back at the wall.

Uh oh.

He froze.

11   Vince Escapes the Lipsticks

It was a tunnel.

WHOOOO.

A dark tunnel of air.

WHOOO.

Whirling round and round.

Coming out of the wall towards him, trying to suck him in.

Vince blinked very fast at it.

He was so busy gaping that at first he didn't notice that his chair was moving.

AAAAGH!

He was being dragged towards the tunnel.

He looked desperately around for help.

The chefs had seen him and were pointing and laughing.

Vince grabbed the table, but his hands couldn't get a grip on the slippery rubber.

AAAAGH!

He was edging towards the wall!

There was no escape…unless…Suddenly Vince took a chance and dived under the bouncing table.

CCCCCCRRRRRRRRR!

Oh no!!!

The sucking force was much stronger under here!

CCCCCRRRRR!

Vince was sucked into a channel of red gooey slime that was running at a tremendous rate towards the wall.

BAH!

He was gulping huge mouthfuls of the stuff!

PAH!

He was spinning!

DAAH!

He was drowning!

And then – Yes!

His hand caught a table leg as it loomed beside him.

He swung up from the channel, legs flying through the air, the force of the wind still trying to suck him towards the wall.

AAAAGH!

He wasn't sure how long he could hold on.

He looked around desperately. There must be something to save him.

Wait.

There were some words scratched into the rubber of the table leg.

It was...it was...it was a sign post!

Someone had been here before him!

Help at last.

He screwed up his nose excitedly to read what it said!

One arrow was pointing back towards the kitchen. "Some…hope," read Vince, suddenly full of strength.

A second arrow was pointing up through the table. "Little…hope," read Vince, feeling a little less energetic.

He slowly turned his gaze to the third arrow. It was pointing straight towards the tunnel. "No…hop".

Hop?

Vince stared at the words.

Whoever it was hadn't even managed to finish the last sentence.

His grip was slipping.

There really was no hope, and –

Wait – what was that?

Something was shooting towards him in the channel.

He screwed up his nose to get a better look.

It was a ball.

It was bouncing over the top of the slime.

Closer.

Closer.

EEEER!

Vince shied away as it began to go past him.

Daaah!

It WAS a ball.

But it was no ordinary ball.

Vince blinked furiously.

It was…he hardly dared think about it.

It was…GULP…GULP… a ball of fingers and thumbs.

It was!

And they were crawling all over each other, weaving in and out of each other as they careered down the channel.

It was like watching a live ball of string!

He craned his neck behind him to see where it had gone.

SHOOOOP!

He was just in time to see it hit the tunnel face and disappear into the darkness.

RCCCCCC!

What was happening now?

RCCCCCC!

The wind was subsiding!

RCCCCCC!

The tunnel was shrinking!

RCCCCCC!

Back into the wall!

RCCCCCCCCCCCCCC!

CLUMP!

Two rubbery doors closed and it was gone.

12 Vince has got Clever Clothes!

BUMPF.

Vince crashed into the slime as the wind dropped completely.

EEEEEEEEE

A tiny shrill scream was coming from inside the wall.

Vince stared at it, breathing heavily. He was soaked to the skin. He wished he was back in his bed.

He pulled his knees into his chest and flopped his forehead onto them.

SCHWEEEEE!

BOOOF!

Ugh!

That was a new one!

Something in his trousers had bashed him in the face.

Great!

Now his clothes were against him.

He opened one eye gingerly. And then opened the other in astonishment.

That "something in his trousers" was a window.

It was.

One of the white squares in his trousers had opened just like a window and a teeny weeny person was smiling encouragingly out at him from it.

And although Vince's teeth were still gritted and his eyes weren't therefore very open, he was sure that this teeny weeny person looked just like him: white hat, white top, black and white trousers!

Vince gasped.

Could this be…his team??

He rolled his eyes.

Typical.

He gets the team who are as big as matchsticks.

Very helpful.

Wait, the tiny person was saying something.

"Hey Vince, my name's Ark. We're the Vincies, here to help you on your mission."

And with that, Vince's trousers went mad. Hundreds of squares flung open to reveal hundreds more tiny people just like the first one. Well, they were all wearing the same clothes as him anyway.

And they all seemed to be living in his trousers!

Imagine that!

Vince stared at them, blinking. He was too amazed to speak.

"Vince! Vince!" Ark's voice brought him out of his daze.

"You've got to get going, Vince! Back into the kitchen and up to that tower!"

Vince blinked at Ark for a moment, and then slowly turned his head to look out at the kitchen from under the table.

Legs running.

Cupboards opening and shutting.

More steam.

More sizzling.

Vince shook his head.

There was no way he was going back out there.

"They'll get me in two seconds," he said flatly.

"No they won't!" yelled Ark. "You've got Sticky Stuff!!!"

Vince turned to look at Ark, and raised his eyebrows at him.

Ark was hanging right out of his window now, waving frantically up at him.

"Come on! Come on! We haven't got much time! Rip off two of your jacket buttons!! They're made of Sticky Stuff. Throw them at the chefs when you get out from under here, and they'll be stuck fast!!!"

Vince was not convinced. He frowned down at his buttons.

They looked pretty ordinary to him.

But the sound of Sweaty McCloud barking orders to the chefs shook him into action. He didn't have any better ideas.

"RARDAR*****!!!!????////RARARARARARARRRRR!"

Vince fumbled for his buttons.

"RARDAR*****!!!!????////RARARARARARARRRRR!"

There they were.

Quickly, he ripped two off and leapt out from under the table.

"RAAAARRRR******"

He was spotted immediately.

Chefs began bouncing and slithering towards him from all sides.

Vince threw one button one way and one another.

POP! POP! POP!

WOW!

The buttons were splitting into more tiny buttons…and more…and more!

POP! POP! POP!

They were scattering all over the floor and shooting off in all directions.

SQUIDGE!!

One of the Red chefs had bounced right onto one and his bottom had stuck fast, just like Ark had said it would!

Vince's eyes sparkled with delight.

The chef writhed on the boingy floor, kicking his arms and legs in the air like a trapped fly.

"Brilliant!" nodded Vince.

SQUIDGE!

Another one was down.

SQUIDGE! SQUIDGE!

And another. And another.

Vince was enjoying this!

"RARRRR****////RRAAAAARRRR!"

Oooh.

Vince turned to see Sweaty McCloud coming for him. He was trying to run but his shoes weren't made for speed. They were too big and they got in the way.

BUMPF!

Sweaty was down in a second, rolling on the boingy floor, sweat flying off him.

And –

SQUIDGE!

He'd rolled onto a button.

"RAAAAR!********************************R!" The roaring, snarling, growling became worse than ever as he kicked and struggled to get free.

WHOOSH!

His silly shoes flew off his feet and floated off around the kitchen.

Oooh – they were all shiny inside.

Vince grinned from ear to ear.

"Wahoo!"

The entire kitchen was full of sticky upside down chefs.

13   Vince Locates the Sess-Pitts

Vince HAD got a great team after all!

"Ark!" he cried, looking from the writhing chefs down to his trousers. "Thanks! Fantastic!"

Wait a minute. There was no one in his trousers. The "windows" were all closed.

If they *were* windows.

"Perhaps I imagined them," Vince wondered, uncertainly.

He shook his head.

He was alone again (apart from hundreds of captured chefs).

He was feeling a bit nervous again.

He bit his lip and pulled himself together.

Right, time to recap on his Mission.

Targets: Sess-Pitts.

Have captured: White chef.

Location: Tower.

Tower.

What tower?

He glanced round the kitchen.

No door, except the one he'd come in through.

No stairs.

He blinked for a minute.

Don't panic.

What about the ceiling?

He looked up. There might be a trap door or…

Oh.

Oh NO!

His jaw dropped.

With the glare of the bright lights over the kitchen counters, he hadn't noticed that there WAS no ceiling at all.

There was just…the sky?

Vince bit his lip.

He peered upwards.

It was very dark. Pitch black in fact.

But…hang on.

It wasn't quite like the night sky at home. He loved looking at that. All deep and mysterious, with stars disappearing higher and higher.

This sky was different.

This sky was a bit, well, flat.

In fact, it looked a bit like the sky they'd made for his school play. Sort of stretched like a sheet above him, and a bit creased.

And there were strange sparkly shapes "stuck" onto it.

Were they stars?

He couldn't make them out.

Vince screwed up his nose.

And – was that supposed to be the moon???

A big silver ball was dangling from the sheet. Slowly it turned one way. Then it turned back the other way.

Vince was confused…but he shook his head.

No time to worry about the sky.

Something else was troubling him more.

Out of the corner of his eye, he'd spotted a tower over to one side of the stretchy sheet.

Hooray!

Trouble was…he'd spotted another one the other side of it.

Hmmmm.

Vince blinked and thought for a moment.

He had a nasty feeling that if...he…turned…round…

He shuffled slowly to face the other way.

He looked up.

He sighed.

It was as he suspected.

Two more towers were looming up into the darkness.

That made four.

This wasn't just a bouncy kitchen.

This really was a bouncy CASTLE KITCHEN!

Now, on an ordinary day in an ordinary place, Vince would have jumped for joy at this discovery.

But this was not an ordinary day.

And Oops is no ordinary place.

So instead, Vince blinked silently at the towers and sank slowly to the floor.

Which tower was the one for him???

14   Vince's Legs Grow Very Long

Vince blinked furiously, trying to pull himself together.

Right.

No point in feeling sorry for himself. He'd just have to get climbing and take a look in the window at the top of each tower in turn.

He looked round the kitchen again.

No doors.

No stairs.

What about the slide he'd arrived on?

No, it was just as slimy as the walls – he'd never make it!

Don't panic!

Don't panic!

He looked around the room.

Of course!

He'd use his Sticky Stuff to climb the walls!

No, wait…

He'd stick fast and never get anywhere.

Don't panic!

Oh, alright, panic!

He slid down the wall and slumped over his knees.

"You've got to get up there," he muttered into his trousers. "You'll never be a true *FYX/it* otherwise. Think. Think!*"

Schweeee.

BOOOF!

Ugh!

His face had been slapped by something in his trousers *again*!

He shook his head and blinked down at them.

Yes! There was another window open, and a new Vincie was smiling up at him, this time sporting a rather large hairy beard.

 "Ah, sorry about that Vince." He looked concerned as Vince rubbed his nose. "I'm Hairy Chops. First name Hairy. Second name Chops. And I can help you get up to the towers."

Vince carried on blinking.

So Hairy Chops carried on speaking.

"You see the button on your trousers, above the zip?" he said. Vince peered down at his tummy and nodded, raising his eyebrows.

"Well," said Hairy Chops. "If you stand up and turn it to your left, your legs will grow. But go easy, you don't want to shoot off too fast."

And with that the window slammed and he was gone.

Vince stared at the closed window, his mouth a little wider open than a second ago.

Did he really say his legs would GROW??

Vince wasn't sure he was happy about that…

Still, he was a *FYX/it*. He had to get up to that White chef. And besides, those other chefs might unstick themselves any minute.

He slithered to his feet and turned the button just a little. Nothing happened. He tried again.

Oh hang on.

Maybe left was the other way. He did get confused sometimes.

Vince gently turned, and… ZZZZZZZZZJJJJJMMMMMM!

WOOOAAAAH!! He shot up into the air!

Vince stopped turning, gasping for breath. He came to a halt, swaying back and forth like a jack in the box. Down at the floor he could just see his feet boinging.

His legs HAD grown!!!!

His trousers were much, much longer than before and as he looked up, he could see he was heading for the funny moon thing.

Vince's face spread into a wide grin. This was going to be fun!

15   Another Lipstick Attack!

ZZZZJJJMMM…ZZZJJJMMMM…

Vince was careful at first, jolting up in little short bursts.

ZZZZJJJMMM…ZZZJJJMMMM

He looked from side to side as he went, but there was nothing much to see – just red slimy walls getting higher and higher.

ZZZZJJJMMM…ZZZJJJMMMM

He was just wondering which tower he would look inside first when –

DING!

What was that?

POW!

Aagh!

Someone had shot him!

POW! POW!

He was hit in the stomach! He bent double with the force.

POW!

Something hit him in the ear!

He was bleeding! Blood was trickling down inside his ear!

Who was this attacker?

He turned to face the wall, groaning.

Daaah!

And leant back in horror!

There in front of him was a dark tunnel of air. Just like the one he had seen under the table.

POW!

Aaaagh!

This time it had got him in the face!

He covered his face with his hands.

Blood! Blood! Everywhere!

He looked down at his hands.

And screamed.

Green blood!!

Green gooey blood!

He was a gonner ! And -

He stopped.

Green blood??

He blinked.

Nothing was actually hurting.

He licked his lips.

Ohhhh.

He licked them again.

Ohhhhhhhhh.

This was no blood.

This was…mmmmm…jelly!!!

That tunnel wasn't so nasty after all!

Mmmm…Mmmmmm…hang on…what was that noise?

WHOOOO

OH NO!!

The tunnel had started sucking again, trying to drag him into the wall!

He'd fallen for its sweet-tasting trick!!

WHOOOO

Vince stuck out his arms and rocked on his huge legs as he tried to resist the force.

OWWWW!

His lips were stretching!

He looked down in horror as they appeared before his eyes, being pulled out towards the wall.

Daaaaah!

And then – oh no!– his hair was going too!

He rolled his eyes upwards to see his fringe hovering like an aeroplane's wing, sucked into a triangle shape, edging closer and closer to the tunnel.

He was going to be sucked up, like Poppet's Dilly Doll when Mum had hoovered it up by accident!

Daaah!

It was no use.

Even his nose was tingling now!

All he could see was the big black hole inside the tunnel.

He'd got to ZZZJJMMMM out of there!

With one enormous effort, he pulled his arms down to his button and turned.

ZZZZ…ZZZZ

He just wasn't strong enough.

ZZZ.ZZZZ..

His lips were about to go in!!

ZZZ.ZZZZ.ZZZZZZZZZZZZZZZJJJMMMMM!

On a mad whim, Vince breathed in as hard as he could, trying to balance the force coming from the other direction.

It worked!

ZZZ.ZZZZ.ZZZZZZZZZZZZZZZJJJMMMMM!

In the nick of time his head shot away from the tunnel and he began whizzing up towards the sky again.

16   Vince Meets Colonel Rouge

What a relief!!

He stopped zzzzjmmming, and breathed out, gulping and gasping.

He looked down below, but there was no sign of the tunnel.

Phew!

He'd fooled it! He'd just rest for a second and then…

Wait.

Rumba. Rumba. Rumba.

Uh oh.

Something was whirring and rumbling in the wall.

Rumba. Rumba. Rumba.

DAAAAAh!

The wall had started to move and…

DING!

NO!!!!

The tunnel was back!

It had chased him up there!

As he ducked away it whirred out towards him and began splurting him again!

SPLURT! SPLURT! SPLURT!

This time, it kept on splurting, and ohhhhh…Vince licked his lips and had to smile.

It was chocolate.

The most yummy, fudgy, melt in your mouth kind.

Mmmmm.

Vince knew it was a trick, but he couldn't move.

He rocked there gently, licking his hands, his arms, whatever he could.

He felt happy and fuzzy. He giggled a bit.

The tunnel kept on spurting.

More. More. More.

Yum.

Ooh. Now the room was swimming.

More. More. More.

Yum.

He could get out of the hole! He was a shark. He was a submarine. He'd fight his attacker with…

"Come in *FYX/it 27*! Come in *FYX/it 27*!"

Oooh. Someone was shouting at him.

LOUDLY.

"Attention! This is Colonel Rouge calling! Do you read me?!"

Vince covered his ears. He thought his eardrums might burst!

"Yes! Yes!" he hollered. Anything to stop the shouting.

But the shouting went on.

LOUDER.

"Come in *FYX/it 27*! Come in *FYX/it*…Oop!"

There was a kafuffle at Vince's knees and the shouting stopped.

Vince peered down dreamily over his nose to see a Vincie dangling from one of the open windows.

"Eh…Ooh…don't worry men…all under control."

Vince wasn't worried – about anything.

Colonel Rouge climbed back inside the window. He was holding a sort of tube with a handle under his neck.

As soon as he was safe, he leaned straight back out of the window and craned his neck up towards Vince.

His face was thin, red and blotchy, with a small black moustache, and half a pair of glasses on his left eye. His jacket was so white, Vince wondered if it might glow in the dark. One arm was covered in medals and stripes.

Colonel Rouge's face lit up when he saw Vince gazing down at him. He quickly pulled the long tube to his mouth and began shouting at him through it.

"Ah, got your attention at last old boy! Got to warn you! Enemy on the left flank! Advance, at the double…quick march…!"

Enemy?

What enemy?

Vince looked at the tunnel in the wall.

That wasn't his enemy! That was his friend!He grinned down at Colonel Rouge and waved.

"'S OK!" he said, his voice a little croaky and slurred. "It's my friend. It's given me some…AAAAAGH!"

WHOOOOOOO!

Vince's hair had shot out towards the wall as the tunnel began trying to suck him in.

WHOOOOOOO!

"Help!" cried Vince, pushing his arms out in front of him, trying to stop the force.

He frowned as far beneath him he saw Colonel Rouge fumbling for something in his pocket and taking a swig out of a flask. This was no time for tea!

The Colonel put the flask back in his pocket, wiped his lips and then began shouting again, louder than ever, through his tubey megaphone.

"I'm ordering you, *FYX/it 27*! You must complete your mission! TO THE LEFT – TURN!!!"

"WHAT?" screamed Vince, his top lip quivering just in front of the black hole.

"TURN THE BUTTON!" squeaked Colonel Rouge, falling forward onto the window ledge and gasping with the effort, his face the colour of beetroot.

Vince finally came to his senses. His legs! Of course!

He gave a mighty yank.

ZZZZZZZZZZJJJJJJJJJJJJMMMMMMMMM.

Oh no! He had turned it much too hard!! He zoomed off like a rocket!

17   Vince's Head Enters the Tower

CLATTER. CLATTER. CLATTER.

Colonel Rouge fell back into Vince's trousers.

Vince didn't see.

In fact, Vince saw nothing. His hair was plastered to his face, covering his eyes, nose and mouth as he shot upwards.

Wind rushed through his ears like the sound of a small aeroplane whizzing up a runway.

RAAAOOOOOOW!

He tried to call for help, but his lips were as dry as sandpaper and he was eating mouthfuls of hair.

"FLUFF-RY-FLIFF!!" he cried.

SMASH!

He had crashed through the kitchen lights.

"FLAFF-MIFF!"

Up. Up.

Towards the towers.

RAAAOOOOOOW!

Up towards that strange moon.

GLINT. GLINT.

RAAAOOOOOOW!

He was nearly up to the windows in the towers.

Ooh. Hang on!

He needed to stop!

"VAFFLIFF SHOFFFA!" he screamed to his Vincies.

No answer.

Vince rolled his eyes.

He looked frantically from one tower to the next.

Choose a tower.

Choose a tower.

RAAAOOOOOOW!

But which one?

Which one?

He could hardly see through his hair and they were all the same anyway!

Tall, red, just one window each, shiny rubbery walls…oh hang on…that one wasn't so shiny.

He looked back round to the one on his left.

Dribbling down its walls was a sort of white gooey gunk.

He'd seen that somewhere before.

Think.

Think.

RAAAOOOOOOW!

Yes! On Sweaty's teatowel! When he'd been ranting about the Sess-Pitts!

Oh yes…yes! That had to be the one!

RAAAOOOOOOW!

He was as high as the tiny window!

Vince blinked at it for a moment.

There was only one thing to do.

Crash land!

He dipped his head and ZZZJJJMMM'd along horizontally, straight towards the open window.

ZZZZZZZZZZZZZZJJJJJJJMMMMMMMMMMM…

He blinked down at his feet far below.

WOOOOOOOOOAAAAAAR

He gritted his teeth and waited for impact.

WOOOOAAAAR…POP!!!!

His head shot through.

SQUELCH!

And stuck fast like a cork in a bottle.

Er…yes, that seemed to have worked.

He'd certainly stopped.

And – EEEEER!

His face was covered in the gooey slime! It had gone up his nose, in his ears, in his mouth!

Daaah!

But he dared not move.

He boing'd there for a moment, eyes shut fast. He smiled a rather silly grin through the goo, in case anyone had noticed him arrive and he needed to make friends.

But nothing happened.

Slowly…very slowly… he opened his eyes.

18   Some Strange Things

AAAAAAGH!

It was an army!

He was surrounded!

All eyes were on him and…

Hang on…

He shook his head.

The eyes didn't have any bodies.

Well, not whole ones anyway.

WHAT???

Vince calmed himself down and looked properly.

O-h-h-h…

They weren't soldiers.

They were pictures.

Hanging all around the walls.

Pictures of…?

Vince screwed up his nose.

Errr…well…Vince picked one close by.

A giant fist.

Giant fist?

Vince stared uncertainly at the picture.

It was!

A fist clenched into a tight ball, two black, beady eyes staring out from it.

Hmmm.

Wait…there were words underneath it.

"Sir Punch Sess-Pitt (1760–1811)," read Vince slowly. Well, at least it looked like he'd come to the right tower.

He read on : "At home at Bunkum Bowels House".

Bunkum what???

Ha!

Vince wanted to laugh.

But he was a serious *FYX/it*.

On a serious mission.

So instead, he nodded and licked his lips.

Bunkum Bowels (snigger) House.

Yes, it was a house. A very, very large house, now that he looked closely at it.

Vince raised his eyebrows.

With zillions of pillars, arches, windows, turrets, statues, lions, tigers, flags…

Ooof! Time to move on.

He glanced at the next picture.

This was much bigger, running right up to the ceiling. And it was of…two …noses.

Vince blinked again.

They were facing each other, nostril to nostril. The nose on the left had a huge boil on the end of it, which oozed like a black volcano. The nose on the right was oozing from the nostril: green slime with pea-sized lumps in it.

Vince thought he might be sick.

To take his mind off it, he looked down at the name plate.

"Wart and Grolly Sess-Pitt," he read.

EEEEER.

Perhaps it would be safer to look at the names instead of the pictures. Find something helpful.

"Spew," he read. "Eeer…Bunnyon…" Vince was trying not to imagine the pictures… "Pong…Natterlie!!!!"

He looked upwards with excitement.

Natterlie Sess-Pitt!

That's the name Sweaty had said!

Oh no!

The picture was hidden behind a huge white gunky splodge.

In fact…most things were covered in that white gunk.

Vince looked round, confused, and then…

Wo-ah…

"Don't look down, Vince!! Don't look down!"

He quickly swung his head back up to the pictures.

Ooh, it was a big drop!

Oooh! That was a big old hall down there!

Vince swallowed.

He had to do it.

He looked down a bit.

Oooh…OK, more pictures.

Big pictures.

Little pictures.

Down. Down.

Straight pictures.

Ooh, wallpaper peeling. Eeeer.

Wonky pictures.

Down. Oooh, too much. Up a bit.

More pictures.

Picnics.

Corgies.

Shoes.

Handbags.

Gold, silver, wooden, cobwebbed frames.

Square, circular, rectangular, triangular *(triangular???)* frames.

Down. Down.

More. More.

Oooh, something different!

A faded, splodged shield.

"V-O-S F-A-C-E-R-I-T" Vince read, spelling out the words scrolled along the bottom.

What did that mean?

He blinked for a moment.

He didn't really want to think about it.

He carried on, past a crack in the wall.

Sticky chandeliers!

Wow!

Covered in cobwebs.

Eeeer…

More pictures. More pictures.

Suit of armour!

Fantastic! Fantastic!

Wo-ah! The floor!

STOP!

Vince's eyes hit the floor with a jolt.

19   Something Rather Disgusting

It had probably been a carpet one day, but whatever was on the floor now looked more like the mush he had trodden in by accident on his school trip to the farm.

Vince retched and turned his attention to the rest of the room.

Well, hall.

Well, stadium.

Well, Vince just didn't know how to describe it.

It was quite simply the hugest room he'd ever set eyes on. He couldn't even see right to the other end. It just melted into a dark murky blackness.

Hmmm.

Stretching along the middle, into the distance, a long, long table was laid for dinner.

There was just one bowl and a rather large chair with gold legs at Vince's end.

There were a couple of candle sticks, but they'd fallen over, and made a mess all over the cloth.

A red mess.

And now Vince could see there were red splodges all over the floor, making a trail like some huge red snail had been crawling around the room.

Vince was getting nervous.

Where were all these red and white splodges coming from?

He continued searching for clues.

What else was there?

A huge golden vase next to the fireplace…a table with a soft green top and fingers lying scattered on it… another table full of more pictures (no surprises there)…

Wait a minute…

Vince swung his gaze back to the first table.

He screwed up his eyes.

Were they really…fingers…???

Vince pulled back towards the window.

He blinked a few times. He remembered the ball of fingers he'd seen under the table in the kitchen.

Suddenly he didn't want to be in Oops anymore.

He tried to squeeze his head back through the window but it was wedged there.

His feet slipped and skidded on the floor way below as he tried to manoeuvre it out.

Daaaah!

And wait.

Oh no!!!

Rumba. Rumba. Rumba.

A Lipstick was coming!

Rumba. Rumba. Rumba.

Where was it? Where was it?

C-R-A-C-KK!

Vince looked down towards the fireplace, which suddenly seemed to be falling apart.

C-R-A-C-KK!

Splinters of marble were flying everywhere. The side pillars had caved in. Something was bursting out from inside.

It was spinning very fast.

It was long and dark.

DING!

Aaagh!

Vince held his breath.

Nothing.

No whooing or sucking winds?

Nothing.

Vince bit his lip nervously, waiting.

And then from inside the whirling tunnel, there came a new noise.

"MEMEMEMEMEMEMEMEMEMEMEMEME"

It was a low sort of humming sound.

"MEMEMEMEMEMEMEMEMEMEMEMEME"

What was it??

"MEMEMEMEMEMEMEMEMEMEMEMEME"

It was getting louder!

"MEMEMEMEMEMEMEMEMEMEMEME....SCHLURRRP!"

EEEER!

SCHLURRRRRP!

EEEEEEEEER!

A gigantic, hideous, red, slug-type thing had squeezed itself out of the Lipstick and flopped heavily onto the rug in front of what was left of the fireplace.

20   Natterlie Sess-Pitt has a Bath

Red gooey slime spattered the walls.

SPLUNCH!

EEER!

A rank smell of mouldy vegetables wafted up to Vince.

DAAAH!

And then an ear piercing shrieking filled the room.

"Ooooof!"

The slug was speaking.

To the Lipstick, apparently.

"That was an uber quick ride up! Thank you SO much, darling! Fabulous! Go now."

"Very good madam," whispered the Lipstick in a low hushed voice.

DING!

The tunnel shrunk back into the wall, leaving no trace in the wrecked fireplace.

As soon as the Lipstick had gone, the slug began humming again.

 "MEMEMEMEMEMEMEMEME…Stupid McCloud," it squawked. "MEMEMEMEME…Can't even keep his staff on their feet!"

Ooh. It had seen the chefs! Vince screwed up his nose.

"MEMEMEME…And he dares to call *me*, *Lady* Natterlie Bella Sess-Pitt, an 'ugly pair of flannel shoes!'"

The slug was drooling and spitting red goo everywhere.

 "MEMEME…that's rich coming from him!…MEMEME…I'll show him what beautiful is…MEMEME."

Vince's jaw was wide open.

This was Natterlie???

SCHLURRRRP.

Natterlie began sliding heavily across the floor, leaving a fresh trail of slime behind her.

SCHLURP…MEMEMEMEMEMEME.

She was heading for the golden vase.

SCHL-U-U-U-U-R-P.

SMACK!

She had heaved herself over the edge of the vase and flopped into it!

G-U-S-SSSSSSSSH!

A wave of thick red goo rushed over the side of the vase and all over the floor.

"HAAAAAAAAGH…" The sound of happy sighing filled the room.

Vince watched in horror as the slug rolled around, letting waves of slimy goo wash over it.

MEMEMEMEMEMEMEME…Vince gasped. There was a hole in the slug! It was opening and shutting as it hummed.

In fact…Vince blinked very fast.

In fact, Natterlie wasn't a slug at all.

Natterlie was…he swallowed…a gigantic pair of slimy, disgusting lips!

21 Spew Makes an Entrance

"HAAAAAAAAGH…"

Natterlie was loving her slimy gooey vasey bath.

EEER!

And now she was heaving that blubbery body back over the side of the tub.

F-L-O-P!

Gallons of red stuff swelled out all over the floor as she landed.

Natterlie ignored the mess, and began moving slowly towards a row of mirrors on the wall.

As she approached, one mirror began to open.

Vince's jaw dropped at what came next.

From behind the mirror came a giant arch of brushes.

On wheels.

And as they approached Natterlie, they began to whir.

VVVVVVVVVV.

Natterlie began sighing again in delight as the brushes began massaging her all over, smoothing the goo as they went.

"MEMEMEMEMEMEME…" she drooled. "Make me shineeee…" She was dribbling again. "Make me glosseeee…make me…"

She stopped.

She was looking in the mirror.

Vince froze.

She'd seen him.

She must have done!

He was doomed!

And then, she…chortled.

Chortled???

"S-p-e-w…" she cooed, teasingly. "Are you in here???"

Vince, who had closed his eyes tightly awaiting attack, opened one eye.

What did she say?

As if to answer his question, Natterlie spoke again.

"Spew…you cheeky little monkey! You've been splodging on my mirrors again haven't you sweetie ! I can hardly see myself! Where are you hiding darling? Naughteeeee...MEMEMEMEME."

The Lips began motoring a little bit faster.

PHEW! Thought Vince, she hadn't seen him after all! But who was… Spew?

Spew…Spew….hang on…wasn't that one of the names on the wall???

And as he thought, something on the wall actually began to move.

He looked across.

It was a splodge on one of the pictures.

Globs of white gunk dripped slowly from it.

"Oh, there you are sweetie!" cooed Natterlie, wibbering up at the splodge. "Have you been having a snooze darling?"

By now the splodge was making its way down the wall.

All that was left in the picture frame was a wet stain above the golden words "Spew Sess-Pitt".

EEER!

Spew WAS a splodge!!

Spew looked like one of Poppet's pom pom balls after she'd been sick on it.

Vince swallowed hard. This was all a bit too weird, even for Oops.

"Come down and give me a kiss darling!" Natterlie was wibbering again.

At these words, the Splodge stopped sliding and began bouncing more energetically onto the picture frames.

SPLIT!

EEEER!

A painting of a rather thinner looking Natterlie perched on a pony, holding on with teeny weeny arms and legs, disappeared behind Spew's white goo.

SPLURDGE!

He'd moved on to a gilt-framed picture of a mop of hair in a blazer and cap.

SPLAT!

"Careful Spewey darling!" shrieked the Lips a little more loudly. "Mind your school picky-wicks!"

Too late!

SPLIT! SPLAT!

"Mind the vasey-wasey!"

Judder. Judder.

A vase on a tall stool wobbled dangerously.

"Spewey! Noooo!"

BOING!

CRASH!!!!!!

Spew had picked up a lot of speed as he had careered down the wall.

As he bounced onto the floor like a heavy porridgey tennis ball, china plates began crashing down from a shelf.

SMASH!

SMASH!

SMASH!

Natterlie blubbered for a moment.

Spew splodged silently on the floor.

Then Natterlie began humming again.

"MEMEMEMEMEMEMEMEME…Never mind angel. It's not your fault. Uncle Wart was right, we should never have brought the best china into a bouncy castle. Come on, sweetie, give me a kiss."

22   Vince Locates Racamoni

Vince shrank back in horror as Spew wiped his slimy porridge all over Natterlie.

"MMEMEMEME…lovely…goooey…fabulous! Now, stay there darling. I'm going to carry on with my game of Snap in a minute, but I need to speak to Racamoni first...MEMEMEMEMEME…"

Natterlie blubbered over towards the wall directly beneath Vince. As he peered down he could see that along it ran a row of huge glass cases.

WOW!

Even from such a long way up, he could clearly see what was in the first case. It was a huge silver spoon, the biggest one he'd ever seen. It filled the whole case.

"MEMEMEMEMEME," purred Natterlie as she slid past. "Hopefully be using you later when my food finally arrives."

BUMP.

"Ooops!"

Natterlie had blundered into the next case.

The lid sprang open.

"Oh sorry darling! Sorry Great Aunt Mildew!" blubbered Natterlie.

CHINK. CHINK.

What was inside?

CHINK.

Vince craned his neck.

Bottles. Hundreds of them. Tiny, pretty glass bottles, in all shapes and sizes.

They seemed to be jostling one another, almost jumping out of the case.

And then one actually did!

Well, it rose up on an arm, sitting on an outstretched hand.

EEEER!

The arm was thin and scraggy with bones sticking out of it. The fingers were gnarled and twisted like roots of a tree. And they were covered in dark green slime!!

YUCK!

The hand thrust the bottle towards Natterlie.

"Oh darling! I couldn't! It's a bit early…" she said.

The hand thrust towards her again.

"Oh, go on then!" wibbered Natterlie, and opened up her big black hole.

Vince shied away in disgust as the bottle began spurting a green liquid into Natterlie's mouth.

"Mmmmm…delicious! Gorgeous!"

Vince retched as the smell of sprouts rose up to his window.

"Thank you darling!"

Natterlie was moving on to the third case.

Vince screwed up his nose.

What was inside…?

No!

His eyes grew wide with terror.

No!

It couldn't be!

It was!

It was a…a…skeleton!

Lying flat in the box.

It had a large golden plaque above it.

"First Pitting," read Vince, terror creeping all over him. "December 1800."

Vince really thought he might be sick.

But wait, Natterlie was already past that one and onto the next.

Oh no – not another skeleton!

Actually, no, not another skeleton.

But it *was* a person.

He squinted just a tiny bit more…and his heart sank.

Squeezed into one of the cases, her nose squidged up against the glass, was a chef wearing a white hat. She was lying flat out, her feet wriggling madly, her arms folded across her tummy.

Vince swallowed hard as he remembered Polly Smart's words:

"Only *FYX/its* can outpitt the Sess-Pitts."

Suddenly Vince wasn't sure he was up to the challenge.

23 Anyone for Sess-Pitt Snap?

As Natterlie approached the final glass case, the chef turned as red as a tomato and began opening and shutting her mouth furiously. Her lips rubbed up and down against the glass.

"MIFFNIFFWIDFFMIFFF!"

Natterlie laughed a loud, nasty laugh. There was no trace of the cooing Spewey voice anymore.

"MEMEMEMEMEMEMEMEMEME …hahaha! What was that you said, Racamoni????"

With a grunt and a snort she was upon the case, sliming all over it.

"MEMEMEMEMEME…Now you listen to me!" she screeched. Racamoni's mouth stopped moving for a moment, glaring at Natterlie, her eyes black with anger.

"Seems one of your team's gone a bit loopy, Racamoni." The Lips were racing so fast, Vince could hardly make out what Natterlie was saying. "Got the Wobble wrong – just like you – and now, he's trying to escape. Well, I've set the Lipsticks onto him, so he should be joining you soon. HA!"

Vince's (by now very long) knees began to knock. The Lips began motoring again.

"And that means, if I don't get my jelly by the next bell, I can play Sess-Pitt Snap with BOTH of you!!! Fabulous! Give old Hopeless a break."

Racamoni poked her tongue out at Natterlie and then started shouting once more.

"MIFFNIFFWIDFFMIFFF!"

"Hopeless?" thought Vince. "Who's Hopeless?" He began reading the labels on the pictures all around.

But Natterlie was moving on.

BOOM!

She had crashed to the ground from the glass cabinet, and was heading for the green-topped table – and the pile of fingers!

"MEMEMEMEMEME…where is she?"

The sickly, cooey voice was back.

"Hopeless?" she sang. "Where are you, darling? Sweaty said you were hiding in his kitchen, but the Lipsticks brought you home. Lovely! Now we can play together again!"

Silence.

"Oh come on Hopeless!" there was less coo and more boo this time. "What's the point of having a sister if we can't play a nice game of Snap once in a while???"

The sound of clicking and clacking came from underneath a velvety chair next to the fireplace.

"Oh stop moaning and come out of there!" shrieked Natterlie. "MEMEMEMEME…I've got your other fingers here… Yes, yes, and the thumbs, we'll put them all back when we've finished."

There was a silence.

And then, something began to roll across the floor.

It was the ball Vince had seen under the table!

And now Natterlie had seen it too. She shot something long, thin and rubbery towards it.

The something unrolled itself at lightning speed across the floor.

It was like a frog's tongue, only a zillion times longer, thicker.

And on the end of it was one, sharp, glinting diamond.

The diamond speared the ball and in a second the tongue had whipped it back towards Natterlie.

Vince gave a little yelp of fear. Fortunately the ball was clicking far too loudly for Natterlie to hear him.

She wrestled the ball onto the table.

"Right!" She was shrieking with impatience. "MEMEMEME… Let's play!"

She was drooling more than ever with excitement. With a lash of her sparkling tongue she whipped up the dice that was sitting on the table and threw it back down next to Hopeless.

"MEMEMEMEMEME…SIX!!!" she was beside herself with glee. "One…snap… two…snap…three..."

Vince really did think he might be sick.

Natterlie was snapping off Hopeless' fingers.

She was!

He blinked at her game for a moment.

No…No…He shook his head and looked back at the glass cases.

He had a nasty feeling that if he didn't rescue Racamoni pretty fast, Natterlie would snap her fingers and thumbs off too!!!!

24   Vince's Cover is Blown

SQUEAK! SQUEAL!

Vince screwed up his face, trying to block out the noises coming from Hopeless, but before he knew it, there was a new commotion in the room.

Ding.

Rumba. Rumba. Rumba.

Natterlie gave a glug of delight! "Oooh! Something's coming after all! Food! Bravo!" she shrieked. "That idiot McCloud's sorted his kitchen out at last! You may be in luck Racamoni!"

She sent Hopeless crashing to the ground and began heaving herself towards the dining table.

Rumba. Rumba. Rumba.

C-R-A-C-KK!!

The Lipstick had reappeared at the fireplace.

"Madam," it whispered.

"Well?!" wibbered Natterlie scornfully. "Where's my jelly??"

"Forgive me, Madam," the Lipstick whispered, "There is no food, but He is here…behind you, up at the window!!"

No!

Slowly Natterlie turned towards Vince.

He smiled weakly.

"Hello," he croaked. "Er…just 'popped' in to… say …er…hello…" his voice trailed off into nothing.

He could almost hear his fingers and toes being snapped off already.

25   Vince's Head Escapes the Tower

GNASH. DROOL. SLURP.

Although she had yet to speak, Vince thought it fair to assume that Natterlie wasn't very happy.

WIBBER. DRIBBLE. SLATHER.

Yep.

As she rocked and foamed below him, he tried again to force his head back through the bouncy tower window.

No luck.

And now Natterlie had begun screeching orders to the Lipstick.

"EAT – HIM!!!"

What???!!

WHOOOO.

Oh no.

Vince recognised that noise.

The Lipstick in the fireplace was trying to suck him in!!

DAAAAH!

He gritted his teeth as his face was pulled towards it.

AAAAAGH!

But wait!!

Something was happening to his back!!

CHING! CHING!

Oh NO!!!

He looked at his shoulders. They had been captured by a red stringy net!

He looked frantically from one shoulder to another.

It was trying to pull him backwards, out of the window!!!

Aaaaagh!

He was trapped from in front and behind!!

And it seemed the force from behind was even stronger than the Lipstick.

AAAAAGH!

All Vince could do was hope for the least worse fate – whichever one that was.

SPUUPPPPUPPPPP!

And it seemed the net was winning.

Those terrible screeching Lips disappeared as his face began shuishing backwards and his eyes were squashed shut.

Naaaaah!

His lips were flattened right up to his nose!

And then…POP!

He sprang out of the window and rocked like a jack in the box under that bizarre, black sky once more.

He whooped for a moment and then remembered that he still didn't know who – or what – had been pulling him.

He didn't want to turn around.

But hang on.

As he boing'd silently, other voices were whooping just like him, and ooh...the straps were pulling a bit again and…

Daaah! Oooh! Aaah!

Suddenly tiny feet were landing on his shoulders, his belt, his shoes way down below.

It was the Vincies!

They'd pulled him out!!

26   Stodgy Dumpling is Cooked

The Vincies were jumping up and down on Vince, slapping each other on the back and doing victory jigs.

Vince jigged with them for a minute, and then spied Ark in his left shoulder.

"Hey, how did you manage that?!" he yelled.

"With these!!" laughed Ark. Vince squinted further along his shoulder and saw hundreds of thin red strings flapping on his top.

"We wrapped them round you, and then round the opposite tower, and all swung on them at once. It was great fun!"

Vince nodded.

"But where did you get them??" he frowned suddenly. "What are they??" They seemed to be sticking to his top leaving red slimy traces.

"It's spaghetti!!" cackled Ark. "Stodgy found it in a cupboard."

"Stodgy?" Vince raised his eyebrows.

"Yeah, Stodgy Dumpling. He likes his food," joined in Hairy Chops.

"So where's Stodgy now then," asked Vince, trying not to laugh.

But there was no time for anyone to answer.

Rumba. Rumba. Rumba.

A Lipstick was coming.

Rumba. Rumba. Rumba.

Where was it??

They all looked around frantically.

"There!" shouted Vince.

The wall of Natterlie's tower was rippling.

A tunnel was opening.

Nobody breathed.

And then –

"POO-EE!!" cried Hairy Chops, waving his hand in front of his nose.

And he was right. A rush of hot mouldy vegetable smells was racing out of the hole.

DAAAAAH!

EEER!

THAT'S DISGUSTING!

As Vince held his nose, the Vincies began jumping back into their squares in his trousers.

SLAM. SLAM. SLAM.

The windows slammed shut.

Vince's eyes were watering, but he didn't need to see. He knew that smell. And he could hear Natterlie gnashing and drooling.

"I – WANT – MY – JELLY!" shrieked Natterlie from inside the Lipstick. "BEFORE – THE NEXT BELL – OR …"

There was a shout from down in the kitchen.

Natterlie stopped jibbering.

Vince stopped shaking.

He looked down.

And rolled his eyes.

It was one of his Vincies.

Stodgy Dumpling, judging by the size of him.

And he'd fallen out of a cupboard into the yellow bowl.

Which was now jigging around like mad.

Windows began opening in Vince's trousers.

SCHWEE. SCHWEE. SCHWEE.

"We've got to get him out!...He'll be eaten! We've got to stop the bowls!"

Vince slipped and slithered as his long legs tried to kick the bowls off the tables. But the bowls were stuck fast to their places.

PUP!!

Oh no!

Stodgy – well, it must have been Stodgy, but he was now covered in green gunk – had been flung from the yellow bowl into the green.

"MEN – SPOONS!!!" barked a voice from his trousers.

And before Vince knew it, his Vincies were flicking tiny red balls at the bowls.

CLINK.CLANK.CLINK.

The balls pinged off the yellow bowl.

"What are you doing???!" yelled Vince.

"If we pierce the bowl, it'll deflate!!" replied Ark, flicking like mad.

Vince blinked down at the chaotic scene below.

This was never going to work, but then…

FFFSSSSSSSSSSSSS!

Yes!! They'd made a hole.

The Vincies threw their spoons in the air and cheered.

But wait – PUP! They were too late! The green bowl just managed to flick a crispier looking Stodgy into the red bowl, before fizzling into a flat rubber mess.

No!!!

The Vincies stared silently at the red bowl which jiggled more ferociously than any of the others.

Their spoons lay on the floor far below where they had thrown them.

Vince covered his eyes with his fists and shook his head in despair.

It was no good.

WOOP.WOOP.WOOP.

Stodgy was in the white bowl now.

SCLUCH.

SCLUCH.

Vince winced as strange gurgling noises came from it. Then, after a few seconds, a floppy sludge of stuff was catapulted from the bowl into the waiting whir of the Lipstick.

The tunnel shrunk back.

The doors closed in the wall.

Stodgy was gone.

There was a moment's silence in the kitchen, and then…

HA! HA! HA! (Ooh! the smell of rotten vegetables!)

Natterlie was cackling evily from her Lipstick up high.

"Aaah…now I've got a little chef to go with my big chef. Two chefs for Sess-Pitt Snap! Fabulous!" she snorted. "Jelly by the bell. Or else!"

27 Vince has a Good Idea

Vince fumbled wildly with his trouser button.

ZZZZJMMMMM.

Daaah! Up! Wrong way!

He couldn't make his legs go down!!!

He'd no idea when that stupid bell would ring and no idea how he was going to rescue his team, but he had a pretty good idea that he wouldn't be able to do much if he was stuck up in the air like this!

"VINCIES!!"

No reply from his trousers.

"VINCIES! HELP!"

The Vincies were still staring forlornly down at their spoons.

Ark looked up sadly.

"How do I get these stupid legs to go DOWN!!!" yelled Vince.

Ark bit his lip.

He smiled a weak smile.

"Ah," he said slowly.

"What?!" yelled Vince.

"Down is…"

"YES!"

"Down is the bit we hadn't quite worked out," finished Ark, speaking very quickly, hoping maybe Vince wouldn't hear.

Vince just blinked at him very, very hard.

Had there ever been a more rubbish team than his White chefs???

Eventually, he said, very quietly: "Well, you'd better get working, hadn't you?"

For the next few minutes, Vince and his helpers twisted, tweaked and bashed his button.

Then a new voice said: "Oh let Stodgy be snapped. He could do with losing a bit of weight anyway."

Vince frowned and looked down at his belt.

It was a Vincie. And he wasn't doing anything at all. He was just lounging on Vince's trouser belt, combing his sleek brown hair and looking into a little hand mirror.

His skin was white as snow, with freckles and a tiny pointy nose above very rosy lips. His jacket had...Vince screwed up his nose to be sure...frills on its sleeves!

He was still combing his hair.

Vince was just about to tell him what he thought of him, when there was a tiny tinkling sound and the Vincie pulled out some sort of phone that Vince couldn't see. He began to talk into it in hushed tones.

Vince's frown deepened, but there was no time to investigate further, as suddenly...WO-AH!

Down he went!

No trouble seeing this time! His hair stood straight on end as he fell.

Ark's proud voice shouted up to him: "It's simple, don't know how we missed it at first. It's a mjzzz, not a zzzjm, if you want to reverse."

"MH-AT?!" mustered Vince. It was difficult to talk, and he couldn't hear through a loud flapping noise, like someone was flapping a newspaper around him. Oh. It was his lips being blown all over the place by the upcoming wind.

"Mhat?" he managed again.

"You turn the button from INSIDE if you want to shrink back down. Ha! Ha!"

"Might," flapped Vince weakly. "Manks."

MJZZZZZZZZZZZZZZ.

As he went, Vince thought about what to do. First off, he'd need to make sure those Lipsticks couldn't get him. He looked nervously at the walls. He'd worked out that as long as he stayed vaguely in the middle of the kitchen, their forces weren't strong enough to reach him. But what about when he was at the cupboards?

Hairy Chops had read his mind.

"Vince!" he yelled up from his rapidly diminishing window. "Don't worry about the Lipsticks by the way. We'll Airyfairy them if they get close to you."

Vince sighed and blinked straight ahead of him for a moment as he descended.

No, he wouldn't ask for details. He'd rather keep his hopes up.

Oooh.

MJZZZZZZZZZZZZZZZ. BOING!

He shook his head.

He'd landed.

He looked down at his legs and wagged his knees a bit.

Seemed to be back to normal.

Vince nodded happily and then looked up.

Right. Ooh. The kitchen was a bit of a mess.

There were the chefs, all still stuck fast on their bottoms, legs waving in the air.

Good.

But…

Pans were bubbling over.

Whisks were whizzing in mid air.

Ovens were overheating; fridges were defrosting.

Machines were spinning out of control and jumping around the room.

Hmmm.

"You!"

Sweaty had spotted Vince and was yelling at him from the floor.

"You have ruined my kitchen! My reputation is in tatters!"

CLINK.

There was a sliding sound from the wall as one of the stars on Sweaty's star chart slipped a little towards the floor.

Sweaty looked quickly across at it, and then began sobbing again.

"Aaaagh!" he cried. "You are smellier than the smelliest piece of cheese on my shoe!!"

If he hadn't been so scared, Vince would have laughed. But he was scared. VERY. So, instead, he blinked nervously at Sweaty, fiddling with his jacket buttons.

Never mind him. He can't move. Think. Think.

How could he make a jelly that would finish Natterlie off?

He'd go and look in a cupboard for ideas.

Daaah!

He couldn't take his hands off his buttons.

Of course!

They were Sticky Stuff!

Vince grinned.

OF COURSE!!!

That's what he could put in the jelly!

He'd stick those Lips together for ever!!!

Prepare for a "Vince Special"!

No.

A "27 Special"!

Vince liked the sound of that!!

28   Vince Makes a "27 Special"

Vince thought quickly. Right.

When he first arrived, they were making Brussels sprout flavour jelly.

EEEER.

So, he'd better make that flavour again.

With one great YANK, he wrenched his fingers from his buttons and raced to the vegetable rack in the kitchen.

Daaaah!

No!!!

WOOOOO

The vegetables were by the wall and a Lipstick was already waiting for him!

But what was that noise…?

PSSSSSSSH!

He turned to see Hairy Chops racing towards the wall holding a tiny strange machine. It looked a bit like the squirter Vince's grandad used on his plants. It was firing steam towards the Lipstick.

PSSSSSSH!

"No-o!" stuttered the Lipstick in its husky voice. "You'll dry me out! No –!"

And it shrank back into the wall at once.

Vince's jaw dropped open.

Hairy Chops came bouncing and slipping back towards him, grinning widely.

He opened his mouth to speak, but Vince interrupted him.

"I know, I know," he said, nodding. "It's an Airyfairy. Well done!"

And he boing'd over to the vegetables.

And stopped.

Daaah!

There WERE no Brussels sprouts left!!!

He hunched his shoulders.

Now what would they do?????

Hairy Chops was at his belt again.

"Vince, Vince," he called excitedly.

"Oh, what?" said Vince, grumpily.

"We can make a chocolate jelly!" cried Hairy Chops.

Vince sighed and looked down at him.

"How?" said Vince wearily. "By asking a Lipstick to spurt us some???"

"Aha!" laughed Hairy Chops. "No, but we can use THIS!!"

He jumped back into his window and then – SCHWEEEE – appeared at another.

He began squeezing something through it.

EEEEEEEE!

Oooh, it was big.

EEEEEEEE!

Surely it would never fit through!

EEEEEEEE – POP!

Vince raised his eyebrows.

It was a huge, red, rubbery jar.

"I found it in Stodgy's room!" yelled Hairy. "He must have collected it when the Lipsticks were spurting!"

Vince could have given him a big kiss (but he didn't).

Instead he grabbed the jar and bounced back to the table.

"Brilliant!" he cried. OK, it wasn't Brussels sprouts, but, hey, everyone loves chocolate don't they? Natterlie will probably be even more pleased to see a chocolate flavour jelly!

He nodded and placed the jar in his pocket.

Now, what about some jelly then???

He ran along the table, looking in all the bowls – aaah, the cubes were already there, in the red bowl.

OK.

He was ready.

And just as well, because.

DINGALING!!!

The yellow bowl had started jigging.

Daah!

Vince began sliding and bouncing back towards it!

"Get off!" he yelped, as he slid across Sweaty who tried to grab his legs.

"Do it properly!" Sweaty was begging. "This is Sweaty McCloud's kitchen! We melt our chocolate over a saucepan first. PLEEEEEAAAASE! AAAAAGH! No! Not over a direct heat!"

He beat the floor with his fists and his heels as Vince kicked himself free and ran to the yellow bowl.

He tipped in all the chocolate and it began to melt inside.

CLINK.

The star finally fell from Sweaty's star chart to the floor.

"No-o!" wailed Sweaty. "I'll be flipping burgers next!"

But Vince wasn't listening.

"Spoon! I need a spoon!" he yelled.

Ark arrived at his belt with a springy red spoon, which Vince used to stir the mixture.

DINGALINGALING!

Oh. Oh.

Quickly, Vince tipped the melted chocolate into the green bowl.

Time to add the sticky goo.

One…two…buttons went in.

And straight away turned into sixteen buttons, which stuck together in a huge gooey mass in the chocolate.

Vince grinned from ear to ear.

DINGALINGALING!

Red bowl.

The jelly had already melted inside and Vince tipped his stodgy mess into it.

Tee hee!

DINGALINGALING!

Oh.

Vince looked at the next bowl.

WOOP. WOOP. WOOP.

He'd forgotten about the wobble bit.

He looked nervously at the wall where the usual Lipstick was waiting to take the jelly to the tower.

It would see if Vince didn't do it right.

What could he add??

And WHAT was going on in his pocket?

29   Vince Adds a Finishing Touch

Wriggle. Wriggle. Wriggle. Hot. Hot. HOT.

"This is no time for games!" he yelled in his pocket's direction.

Wriggle. Wriggle. Wriggle. Hot. Hot. HOTTER.

"Ow!" yelped Vince and he danced away from the table. "What IS that in my pocket??"

"Ah, sorry Vince," shouted Hairy Chops, jumping out of it and juggling a very large sweet in a fantastically shiny pink wrapper.

PINK!!!!

Vince blinked down at the sweet.

Pink!!!

He'd forgotten about the jellies! At least, he thought they must have been the jellies once, only…now they'd grown twice, no three times their size, and they were covered with these blinding wrappers, which had…wait…black things running all over it like ants?!

What were they…?

Vince peered in closer.

They were…words!!!

Words??

He tried to catch them as they whizzed past. "Bom….Bom… DaaaH! Too quick!" He blinked and tried again.

Small words were creeping more slowly now.

"Too hot to handle…fiery delight…make your mouth explode…"
Vince's eyes sparkled. His lips drooled.

Wait – there was the big word again.

"Bomb…"

Next time he'd get it.

"BombBurs"

DAAAAAh!

"BombBurster!!!!"

Vince bit his lip.

WOW!

Vince wanted a BombBurster and he wanted one now.

More words were crawling again: "A million sweet sensations…"
he read.

"Vince! Vince!"

"Honey…sugar…"

"Hurry up! VINCE!!"

It was Hairy Chops, who was still jigging around with the sweet in
his hands.

Vince shook his head and stared at Hairy, who smiled and nodded.

Then he raised his eyebrows and in an unnecessarily loud and
slow voice, he said:

 "Add this 'WOBBLE'," he looked over towards the Lipstick, and
then looked back at Vince, winking, "to the jelly and bang, we're
done!!!"

Vince didn't have a chance to refuse.

Hairy had thrown the sweet into his hands.

Ah. Ooh.

It was too hot! It was like holding a volcano! And now it was shaking slightly and making a rumbling noise.

GGGLLLL!

Gritting his teeth and jigging on the bouncy floor, he used the very tips of his fingers to undo the wrapper.

POP!!!! SIZZLE!!!! POP!!!

Three fiery red balls shot out and bounced across the table leaving black singe marks behind them. They jumped into the white bowl and disappeared into the jelly with a loud gurgling sound.

Vince stared silently at the bowl.

He shook his head and closed his wide open mouth.

"Right," he said loudly. "That's the – er – wobble in. Just one more stir, and we're ready."

He bounced back to the bowl. Ooh. An interesting mixture sat bubbling in it.

He crossed his fingers and gave one final stir.

WOOP. WOOP. WOOP.

The alarm was ringing again.

The bowl gave one final jig and then jumped into the Lipstick and was gone.

30   She Doesn't Like Chocolate????

"NNNNNOOOOO!!"

The kitchen was filled with the sound of shrieking and spitting echoing down from the tower through rubbery pipes.

Vince screwed up his nose and put his hands over his ears.

"MEMEMEMEME...NOT CHOCOLATE!!! NEVER CHOCOLATE!!!"

He blinked upwards.

She didn't like chocolate then.

"It's so dirty! It's so messy!"

WHAT???

Vince could hardly believe his ears.

The words continued to echo down.

"White chocolate maybe...the colour of you, darling Spewey, but not this messy sludge...! McCloud! You uber idiot!"

Sweaty groaned and covered his ears.

"MEMEMEMEMEME...COME ON RACAMONI, LET'S PLAY SESS-PITT SNAP FOR REAL!!"

Vince and his Vincies gasped together!

"We've got to stop her!" Vince cried frantically, his head in his hands.

THINK.THINK.

Pitter. Patter. Pitter. Slip! Patter.

What was that?

Vince looked down to see his Vincies charging off somewhere!

Oh great!

Now his team had abandoned him in his hour of need.

Typical.

He looked wildly round the room for an idea.

But what was this coming towards him along the red rubbery table?

He held out his hands in front of his face.

Was this some new kind of Lipstick attacking?

No.

It was getting closer.

It was a long, thin red rubbery thing.

On legs.

It was a monster!

It was a snake!

It was a …a…rolling pin…?

Vince put his arms down and sighed.

A rolling pin being carried by his Vincies.

Right now, he would even have preferred a monster.

He rubbed his forehead with his hand and waited for an explanation.

"We'll roll her flat, Vince!" announced Hairy Chops, grinning from ear to ear.

Vince just stared back.

"And post her away," added Ark (and he was supposed to be the sensible one!).

This had to be their most ridiculous plan yet!

But Vince could hear shouting coming from the tower.

He'd have to consider it.

"Post her away in what??" he asked.

"Your hat, Vince!!" they all yelled together.

Vince yanked his hat off his head and threw it on the table.

"Oh yes!" he mocked sarcastically. "Because a hat's just like an …env…e...lo...IT IS AN ENVELOPE! IT IS AN ENVELOPE!!" Vince was bouncing high on the kitchen floor in excitement.

For when he had laid his hat flat, he could see it had a stamp on it.

And beneath the stamp were some rather fantastic words. Vince read:

> If you know a slimy lady who will only eat jelly,
> Why not send her on a trip to Gorbelly.
> We'll stuff her with food. She'll grow! She'll explode!
> Just post her to the address below:

Gorbelly School,
7 Chubby Close,
Podgesome,
Stout.

Vince looked from the rolling pin to the envelope and back again.

And then his face spread into a very wide grin.

31   Vince's Helicopter Top Explodes

"OK. OK." said Vince, resting his hands on the envelope, and trying to ignore the squeals from above. "We've got an envelope. We've got a rolling pin. But how on EARTH are we going to get those Lips down here??"

He had hardly finished his sentence when a new voice interrupted him.

"Stand back, everyone! This is a job for The Great Vicendo!!"

And with that, a Vincie that Vince hadn't seen before leapt up to the applause of everyone else.

"Tra la la la!" He bowed, and winked at Vince.

Vince peered down at him.

He was a bit of a mess!

He looked a bit like baby Poppet did when she'd finished eating her food.

His long curly hair was black and greasy.

His dark, tanned face was black and greasy.

His chef's jacket was black and greasy. And it was all out of shape too, hanging heavy with things in its pockets.

Vince really couldn't see what use he was going to be, but the rest of the Vincies seemed very excited.

The Great Vicendo began unbuttoning his "white" coat.

"What's he DOING?!" frowned Vince.

"You'll see!" smiled Ark, clapping.

"Tra la la la!" As The Great Vicendo threw off the coat, Vince saw that he was wearing his own helicopter pyjamas underneath it.

"Hey, they're mine!" he shouted.

"Yes," replied The Great Vicendo with a flourish. "And it's time we put them into action!" He tapped his nose, winked at Vince and took a small can from behind his ear. He began squirting something black and greasy at the helicopter on his pyjamas.

"Hey!" interrupted Vince again, as a black and greasy stain seeped everywhere.

The Great Vicendo held his hand up for Vince to be quiet. He put his head on one side and looked down at the pyjamas.

Judder.

He smiled at Vince.

Judder. Judder.

What was that noise???

Judder. Judder. Judder.

Vince looked in alarm at the helicopter. The blades had started turning round!

They had!

And they were turning faster and faster.

SCHWEWWWWW!

Vince and his Vincies covered their eyes as the rush of wind grew stronger.

But not The Great Vicendo.

He smiled broadly and stretched out his arms, bending his body backwards to give the helicopter space.

"STOP!" pleaded Vince. "You're ruining it! You'll…"

POOOF!!!

What was that?

POOF! POOOOF! POOOOOOOF!

Vince peeped through his fingers!

No!!

The helicopter was exploding out of the t-shirt!

POOOOF!

There went the roof!

POOOOOF!

Now two doors!

There'd be nothing left!

Poooof!

It was like watching a huge blow up monster coming to life.

POOOO-OOOOF!

OOOF!

JUDDER. JUDDER. JUDDER.

It was out.

JUDDER. JUDDER. JUDDER.

A gigantic rubber helicopter was hovering before Vince's eyes…

He swallowed.

He didn't know whether to laugh or cry.

It was a fantastic sight.

JUDDER. JUDDER.

But there was a massive hole in his pyjamas and…

Wahooo!

The other Vincies were jumping and clapping with delight.

The Great Vicendo gave a quick bow and then got back to work. He dropped to his knees beneath the helicopter. He grabbed his spanner and began tinkering with something.

"Go Vicendo!" chanted the crowd!

But then –

"Attention!" came a thundering voice through the megaphone. "Attention! Pilot descending!"

Pilot?

The Great Vicendo rolled his eyes upwards to a window in Vince's trousers, from where Colonel Rouge was climbing gingerly down.

"Eh…oooh…" he puffed. "Don't worry men, no need for assistance."

The watching Vincies were shaking their heads up at him. The Great Vicendo had sucked in his cheeks and was twirling the spanner between his fingers.

"Eh…oooh…alright men, officer safely down," yelled Colonel Rouge through the megaphone as he hit the floor.

He stamped his feet together and swung round to face the others.

Wow.

His trousers had creases so sharp you could cut your finger on them.

He frowned at the gaggle of Vincies around The Great Vicendo.

"What's this? What's this??" he megaphoned. "Get back! Get back, men! Fall in! And… ready Colonel! To the left, quick… march."

He lifted a leg and began marching towards them. He instantly fell over on the bouncy floor.

"Oop!"

The sound of sniggering drifted up to Vince. He put his head in his hands. They were wasting valuable time!

And what was happening now?!

Colonel Rouge had recovered himself and was crouching down inches from The Great Vicendo, stuffing the megaphone into his face. "You! Look at the state of you! You are a disgrace to this regiment!!"

The Great Vicendo didn't flinch.

"You can't go into action looking like that!" continued Colonel Rouge. He brought out a tissue, spat on it, and began wiping The Great Vicendo's face.

There was a gasp from the crowd of watching Vincies.

"Right," said Colonel Rouge, trying to push The Great Vicendo to one side. "Fall in! I'll get this old bird off the ground."

But The Great Vicendo had had enough. Without warning, he stuck his tongue out at Colonel Rouge and gave him a gentle shove on the shoulder with one grubby finger.

"Oop!"

BOING!

The Colonel fell backwards and lay flat on his back, arms and legs spread out.

BOING!

"Oop!"

He tried to raise his head.

"Don't worry men…"

He flopped back onto the floor. His voice was fading.

"Permission to fly NOT granted…"

It was only a whisper.

"NOT…"

There was a silence.

Everyone held their breath, but Colonel Rouge didn't get up. In fact, a faint sound of snoring began coming from his direction.

The Great Vicendo grinned and winked up at Vince.

Then with a flourish he leapt into the pilot's seat.

Vince blinked furiously, trying to smile as The Great Vicendo gave him one final thumbs up.

Then the engine roared. The blades shook. And the helicopter flew off towards the tower.

32 Got Her!

Everyone was gazing silently upwards. Vince just blinked straight ahead, his jaw wide open.

Meanwhile, The Great Vicendo wasted no time. He hovered at the tower window for a moment, and then jumped down onto the legs of the helicopter, his lasso in his hand.

Oooh.

A gasp rose up from the Vincies below.

The Great Vicendo beamed down at them.

And then…

SSSSWWWWING!

He swooped the lasso inside the tower.

AaaERERE!

A screech rang out through the kitchen like a squawking parrot.

The Great Vicendo tugged and worked at his rope.

"MIMIMIMIMIMIMIMIMIMIMI" screeched the voice.

Quickly, The Great Vicendo leapt back into the pilot's seat, tied the rope to the door and then flew up towards the moon.

BUMPF. BUMPF.

The tower wall bulged as something heavy bounced against it inside.

Higher and higher rose the bulge.

BUMPF. BUMPF.

The rope was straining through the window.

BUMPF.

Whatever it was, it was nearly there.

BUMPF.

There was a moment's silence and then...

SCHLURP!

Something horribly red and sticky appeared at the window.

Oooh!

The Vincies gasped again and leant back in horror.

SQUISH!

Oooh!

SQUEEZE!

Aaah!

SQUELCH!

Uggh!

As The Great Vicendo revved his engine, the blubbering mass was inching its way out through the hole.

Its veins throbbed and folded into red rivers.

Red slime oozed all over it.

DRIP!

EEER!

Vince rubbed frantically at something gooey in his hair.

SCHLURP!

It was nearly through!

ANGANGANG!

The sound of gnashing and slathering filled the kitchen.

POP!

Vince and his Vincies held their breath.

Natterlie shot out and was dangled beneath the helicopter.

"MIMIMIMIMIMIMIMI"

The kitchen was filled with her shrieking.

"HOW DARE YOU??? DON'T YOU KNOW WHO I AM???
I'M RELATED TO QUEEN VICTORIA YOU KNOW!
MIMIMIMIMIMI!"

The rope was squeezing her tightly in the middle. She bulged out
either side, like a hideous kiss above their heads.

"I'LL GET YOU FOR THIS!"

She was puffing and swelling, fit to burst.

The Great Vicendo beamed and let her struggle there for a while.
And then, all of a sudden, he untied the rope and let it fall from the
helicopter.

The end sailed down past Natterlie. She stopped wrestling
momentarily, to watch it pass by.

And then she began to scream even louder.

"MIMIMIMIMIMIMIMIMIMI"

But there was no hope.

As the rope fell to the kitchen floor, so Natterlie began to drop like a stone behind it.

EEEOOOOO!

Vince covered his face in horror as a red blur of slime, goo and flesh shot towards him.

THUD!!

It crashed heavily in front of him onto the kitchen table, sending globs of greasy red gunk flying everywhere.

SP—LUN—CH!

33   The First Enemy is Defeated

Daah! Yuck!

The Vincies screwed up their noses and began gingerly wiping their splattered clothes with their hands.

Vince was still in shock.

"Er…er…" he stammered.

"CARRY ON! CARRY ON MEN! GOOD WORK! GOOD WORK!!"

Vince jumped.

Colonel Rouge had woken up and was megaphoning again.

Vince looked down at the writhing oozing beast before him.

The Vincies HAD been busy!

They'd already tied Natterlie up with some of that red spaghetti that they'd used to save him earlier.

Natterlie was really angry now, spewing out gallons of foaming red liquid. She looked like one of those parcels his gran sometimes sent him, tied tightly with hundreds of pieces of string.

She was still trying to scream. "MMMMMMMMMMMMM"

Colonel Rouge was standing to one side, megaphone in one hand, flask in the other.

Each time Natterlie jerked and struggled, he skipped back a step.

The rest of the Vincies were preparing to roll.

"ALRIGHT LINE UP! LINE UP! KIT INSPECTION IN TWO MINUTES!" ordered Colonel Rouge.

"No time, Rougey," sighed Ark from his place at the rolling pin. "Come on Vince, let's roll!"

Vince pulled himself together. "OK, after three. One, two, three. Roll!!!"

They started rolling Natterlie out as flat as a book. With a squidge and a squelch, she became a big red mess on the table. In squished some eyes and a nose and some ears.

Where did they come from?

EEER

The kitchen was filled with her loud, shrill screams, but there was no escape.

On and on they rolled.

They stopped briefly to rescue Hairy Chops, whose beard had got stuck under the rolling pin. He was a little bit squashed and a little bit smudgy, but he was OK.

And eventually Vince ordered:

"Enough! I think she'll fit!"

They folded up the rubbery, mish mashy mess and briskly slid it into the envelope.

They licked it down.

It bulged and jumped as Natterlie tried to escape.

Vince gritted his teeth and held it tight.

"She's ready to post!!" he cried. "What do we do now???"

He ducked as the sound of the helicopter suddenly grew louder and a rush of wind filled the kitchen.

The Great Vicendo was at Vince's ear, reaching down from his helicopter legs.

He scooped up the bulging envelope and saluted Vince.

"No problemo," he beamed, and the helicopter disappeared into the moonlit sky.

She was gone.

34 The Second Enemy is Defeated

Vince looked from one Vincie to another in amazement for a moment.

And then, all at once, they began whooping with joy!!!

Weee! Bounce! Boing!

Wait.

What was that???

WHIR. WHIR. WHIR.

The room was suddenly filled with a thundering noise.

WHIR. WHIR. WHIR.

Something was falling. Something was going to crash onto their heads!

Was it the helicopter?

Vince looked up.

Nothing.

He looked around.

Daaah!

It was the walls!

WHIR. WHIR.

Rippling and shaking.

WHIR. WHIR. WHIR.

The Lipsticks were out of control!!

WHIR. WHIR. WHIR. WHIR. WHIR.

Down they plummeted to the ground.

S-W-I-S-H!

For a moment the whole kitchen swayed around them like a pot gone seriously wrong on a potter's wheel.

Woaaaah!

Then all was still.

Everyone held their breath, looking nervously from wall to wall…

And then the whooping began again!

Wahoo!

Weee! Bounce! Boing!

Vince had never been happier!

Oh, but WAIT!!! Now what was THAT noise???

He stopped bouncing, frustrated.

SNUFFLE. SNORT. SNUFFLE.

There was a strange grunting coming down the pipes from the tower.

SNUFFLE.

Were Racamoni and Stodgy in trouble?

SNORT. SNORT.

Vince had forgotten about Spew!!

SNUFFLE.

Without another thought, he began zooming back up to the window.

ZZZZZJJJJMMMMM… ZJJJM… ZZJ…

Cautiously, he peeped over the edge.

EEEER!

Spew was racing round and round the room leaving gooey brown smudges everywhere.

EEEEEER! EEEEER!

Hang on!

Brown smudges?

Vince frowned.

BROWN?

He gasped. Of course!

Spew had eaten the "*27 Special*"!

Yes! Vince watched with delight!

Oooh, no! Vince ducked in horror as from underneath the goo, Spew drew out two long ghoul like arms and stretched them across the floor towards the window.

Daaah!!

Spew was coming for him!

Daaah!

Vince bent as far from the window as he could, waiting for the attack.

BLINK. BLINK.

But instead, there was a new, horrible, moaning sound.

Woaaaaaaaaang!

Vince looked up.

Woaaaaaaaaang!

Vince zzzjjjmmm'd up.

Woaaaaaaaaang!

Vince popped up.

EEEEEER!

Spew was wrestling with something inside his hairy goo.

Yuck!

It was his mouth!

EEEEER!!

It was his teeth!

Yuck!

Yellow and crusty and …oooh…stuck together by his Sticky Stuff!

Hoorah!

But wait, what was happening now?

TINKLE.

A tooth had fallen out!

TINKLE. TINKLE.

And another.

And another.

TINKLE. TINKLE. TINKLE.

Spew moaned and wailed as out they all came.

They bounced onto the floor like hailstones and rain.

Vince screwed up his nose at the black gaping hole left yawning in the middle of Spew.

But there was more to come.

For as Spew splodged in a heap on the floor, the teeth began to shake and rattle in front of him. And from each tooth came more little teeth, and from the little teeth came tiny teeth and from the tiny teeth came tiniest teeth.

Until the floor was covered with them all rattling around.

Spew began to splodge slowly backwards.

And suddenly, the teeth all jumped towards him, with a roar and a snarl.

WAAAAAR!

The teeth had turned into a massive, toothy monster, clicking and clacking over Spew. It looked just like one of the dinosaur skeletons Vince had seen in a museum once.

"WAAAAAAGH!!" Spew let out a terrifying scream. He tried to splodge away some more, but…

BANG!

SPLAT!

Daaah!

What happened there?

Something had splatted all over Vince's face.

SPLIT!

And some more.

EEER!

SPLIT! SPLAT!! SPLOT!!!

Spew had exploded!

Vince's BombBursters had finally taken effect!

There was chocolate EVERYWHERE.

FANTASTIC!

SPLOT!! SPLAT!! SPLIT!! SPLIT!! SPLIT!! SPLIT!!

35 Mission Accomplished

DRIP. DRIP.

A sort of chocolatey goo was dripping and sliding down inside the walls of the tower.

Vince wiped his face and peered through the window.

There was a strange eerie silence.

Where were Racamoni and Stodgy? Their glass case was completely covered in goo. He couldn't see a thing. Had Spew got them before he had exploded????

In answer to his question, the case suddenly burst open.

BANG!

Vince shied away.

There was the sound of someone yawning, and two hands stretched upwards.

Then the two hands grabbed one edge of the case.

Vince braced himself.

A white hat appeared over the side.

Then a mop of black hair.

Then a huge pair of black-rimmed glasses.

Two big eyes peeped out from behind them.

The mop of hair nodded.

Safe.

A finger pushed the glasses back up against the eyes and – wo-ah!
– a pair of check-trousered legs swung over the case, followed by
a very large bottom.

BOING!

Racamoni did a sort of back flip onto the floor.

"Cha!" She scrambled to her feet and pushed her glasses up once
more. She was so short her trousers draped right over her fat little
toes.

She bounced there gently for a moment, clasping her hands around
her middle, her white hat quivering.

And then she started shouting.

"E! Finalementi!!!! Stupiddi lippi snippi fingitti!!" she waggled
her podgy fingers furiously at anyone who might be listening.

And then she spied the monster which was cowering by a wall.

"Oh no," thought Vince, "not the monster, please don't shout at
the monster! He hasn't had his lunch!"

"E! Weirdi doggi!"

Vince groaned and shut his eyes. He couldn't watch. But it seemed
the monster was staying put.

Racamonni wagged a scary finger at it.

"Sitnomovie!"

The monster sat down.

"Vince!"

No! Someone was calling him!

Racamoni swung round to where the voice had come from.

A sort of over-stewed gooseberry, which Vince assumed was Stodgy, was now sitting on the edge of the case, waving up at him.

His cover was blown.

Racamoni turned her gaze up towards him. She pushed her glasses up to her eyes.

"E! fattiti??" she shouted up to him.

Vince raised his eyebrows and smiled a weak smile.

He had no idea what she was talking about.

But Stodgy was answering her anyway.

"Who are you calling fatty!!" he huffed.

Racamoni turned to look at him, clasping her hands more tightly around her middle.

She peered down at him, gave her glasses a shove, and then shook her head, muttering, "weirdi mini shifti".

Before Stodgy could protest, she turned back to Vince and began shouting even more loudly.

"E! Fattiti??!"

Oh no.

Vince's smile faltered.

But help was on the way.

"Wait! Wait!" came a voice from his belt. "She's speaking Titilian, let me translate."

A new Vincie scrambled up Vince's top and over his face.

"Ooh…aaah!" spluttered Vince as his mouth, his nose, his eyes were used as stepping stones.

"OOOOWWW!"

As the Vincie climbed, Vince could just make out a pair of tiny round glasses and some very shabby clothes. There was a button missing from his jacket. There was a hole in his trousers. He smelt faintly of school dinners (yuck!).

The Vincie sat on Vince's head and began flicking quickly through a small book.

"I'm Ken," he said by way of introduction, "Ken Twig. But you can call me Savvie." Vince raised his eyebrows at him. "And what Racamoni wants to know is…" Savvie flicked some more, "did Spew eat all the chocolate?"

Vince nodded energetically.

"Yes, yes," he said. "And now he's exploded. He's gone."

Racamoni shrugged and glared at Savvie for a translation.

"Grandi bangi! Lookti mess!"

Racamoni frowned at him over her glasses, her chin on her chest.

"No spikka Titilian???" she shouted.

Savvie was most offended.

"That IS Titilian!!" he yelled back. "Grandi bangi! Lookti mess!"

Racamoni thought for a moment.

"Aaah," she nodded approvingly, surveying the dripping walls.

"E! Mystifelka loonidipsi?" she shouted.

There was a silence.

"And?" called Vince, straining his eyes up at Savvie.

"Just a minute! Just a minute!" Savvie put up his hand.

FLICK. FLICK. FLICK.

"She's worried about Natterlie coming back."

"Tell her it's OK! Tell her!" said Vince.

"SSSSH!" Savvie was flicking madly…

"Supi wendi ofti," he said finally.

Racamoni sighed and frowned at him over her glasses for a moment. Then she nodded. She began to march in great boings towards the fireplace, which was now just a gaping hole in the wall.

"What's she up to?" asked Vince nervously.

FLICK. FLICK. FLICK.

Savvie flicked though his book.

"Hurry up!" hissed Vince as Racamoni got closer.

"Whati dodi?" shouted Savvie as calmly as he could.

"Backti cucci!" shouted Racamoni. "Bevvi gaspi!"

Savvie's voice came quietly, trying not to sound panicky.

"Er…she says she's going back to the kitchen because she needs a drink."

"OK," said Vince, slowly, "so why is she going towards the fireplace???"

Racamoni's face was in the hole.

"Shutti uppity – stupidi shifti blanci – needi boundi!???"

Her big bottom was disappearing.

"Er…she says, be quiet Vince" said Savvie, "so she can – er – jump."

"Jump!!" Vince's eyes nearly popped out of his head.

Racamoni's voice echoed out from the hole. "Si, boundi. Shutti uppity."

And she had gone.

"WEEEEEE!" her voice echoed round the kitchen as she fell down the shaft made by the Lipstick.

BOING!!!!!!

WEEEEE!

Her laughing face reappeared briefly in the hole and was gone again.

BOING!

WEEEE!

Quieter this time.

BOING!

THUD.

Silence.

She'd landed.

36   Uh Oh

Vince looked quickly down to see Racamoni bounce out into the kitchen, brushing herself off.

Stodgy jumped out of her jacket pocket.

Good thinking Stodgy, thought Vince, and then zzzzjjjjmmmm'd quickly down himself. When he arrived, Racamoni was howling with laughter at the sight of all the chefs trapped on the floor.

"Cha Cha wibbly!" she cackled, wriggling her fingers and kicking her legs.

Vince nodded and wriggled his fingers too.

But then he stopped.

HISSSSSSSSSSSSSSS.

What was that noise???

HISSSSSSSSSSSSSSS.

He looked around him.

Was it his imagination, or was the kitchen getting a bit smaller???

Suddenly there was a commotion at his trousers.

SLAM! SLAM! SLAM!

The Vincies were returning hurriedly to their windows.

"What's going on?" cried Vince.

Ark was one of the last to disappear.

"It was the explosion, Vince. It's made a hole in the tower wall. We're deflating!"

Vince's jaw dropped.

And it wasn't just the walls that were going down. Tables, chairs and cupboards were all starting to droop and wilt.

And – wait – so were those nasty chefs.

Racamoni clasped her hands round her middle and bent double with laughter as their faces grew shrivelled and their fingers waved around like tiny chipsticks.

EEEER!

HA! HA!

Fantastic!

Oh hang on.

Vince stopped laughing.

He boing'd over to the cupboard through which he had entered all that time ago.

NOOOOO!

The slide was deflating too!

He blinked at it and sank slowly to the floor.

How would he get home if there was no slide????

37   The Monster is a Friend!

WEEOOOWEEE!

A high pitched whistle brought him back to his senses.

He sniffed and stumbled back out in to the kitchen.

DAAAAh!

And jumped straight back behind what was left of the door!

The tooth monster had jumped from the tower window and was flying down to the kitchen.

Vince shook so much that his own teeth nearly fell out.

It was gnashing its teeth and looking generally very scary, but Racamoni was whistling and smiling at it.

And then, as the monster landed, it smiled sweetly and swayed its hips at Racamoni.

Vince's eyes nearly popped out of his head.

"Are you ready now then lovie?" it said, in a surprisingly high pitched girlie voice.

Racamoni nodded and then turned to Vince.

"Quickie Skop Hotch!!" she shouted, and beckoned him over.

Vince stayed where he was. This had to be a trick. And anyway, his mum always told him never to accept sweets from strangers (whatever "skop hotches" might be – actually they sounded quite nice).

But wait, what was happening now???

Racamoni was climbing onto the monster's back!!

Was she mad???

And – oh no.

The monster was coming over.

Vince dived away from what used to be the door and tried to hide in the rubbery pile which used to be the slide.

It wasn't a very good hiding place.

He smiled weakly as the monster and Racamoni approached.

"Come on Vince," said the monster. "Skop Hotch is great fun. Especially when you fall off!!"

Vince frowned and rocked on his heels, biting his lip. He always loved a new game, but he still wasn't sure if he could trust the monster. He was in Oops, after all.

Racamoni was getting impatient.

"Gi witouti," she shouted, giving the monster a kick.

"Come on Vince," said the monster. "We're dropping Racamoni off at the Oops beach – she's going to have a holiday. Then I'll take you on home."

At the word home, Vince gave in. What other choice did he have?

Anyway, he was still ready to box the monster's ears off if he needed to.

He jumped up and sprang onto the monster's back.

38   Let's Play Skop Hotch!

"Good-oh," cried the monster, and began bounding across the deflated kitchen.

Wooo-ahh!

Vince held on tightly, burying his head into Racamoni's white jacket.

Then he looked up.

They'd stopped.

That was quick!

But – oh.

They were still in the kitchen.

Vince slid off the monster, suddenly very tired.

They were standing where one of the four towers had once risen high. Now it was just a pile of blubbery rubbery on the floor. But something else rose up in its place.

Vince screwed up his nose.

It was a mini tower. A mini tower made of – well – lots of numbers, jumbled together – ones, twos, threes.

Vince opened his mouth and turned to Racamoni and the monster, who were both looking intently up at the sky.

"It's the Skop Stop, Vince," said the monster, without moving his head. "Got to catch the Number One in order to start."

Vince blinked at him for a moment, and then looked slowly up at the sky.

It was dark. There was that strange moon. Nothing Number One-like.

"Come on Vince," said the Monster. "Come and stand properly at the stop. The more of us there are, the more likely they'll come and get us."

Vince looked at the monster and then back to the sky. He took a step sideways onto the base of the number tower.

And gasped!!!

The moon had started turning round and round. It spingled and spangled like a silver bauble on a Christmas tree.

The sheet-like sky was flapping madly, like people were shaking it from the sides. And one by one, the stars were falling off it.

They were!

And they'd started doing a funny sort of dance around the ball.

ZOOOM.

Forwards.

ZOOM.

Backwards.

Hang on.

Vince screwed up his eyes.

They really were funny shaped stars!

They didn't have enough points. There was a round bendy one. Look, that one was tall and thin.

Vince blinked for a moment, and began nodding slowly.

Now he understood what the monster was on about.

They were numbers.

Tiny shiny numbers.

And they seemed to be whizzing about on silver wheels.

Vince gazed up at them, his eyes wide.

"Any luck Vince?" chirped the monster.

Ooh. Right, back to work.

Could he see a number one?

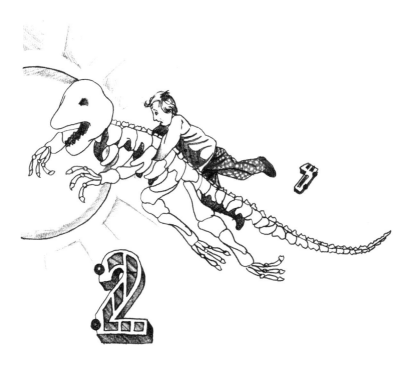

He wasn't sure why they needed a number one, but he'd try and find one all the same.

"Er…2…er…6…er"

The monster was tutting.

"Typical," he muttered. "There's never one when you want one. There'll be three along at once in a minute, just you wait and see…oooh, hang on!"

He started shouting and jumping.

"There's one! There's a Number One! Come on!"

The monster hit a button on the number tower. Disco music began blaring out all around them, and the night sky was suddenly lit with flashes of colour…gold…now green…now pink!

"Come on!" cried the monster again. "We've got to do the best Skop Hop, or someone else will get the bus!"

And he started hopping like crazy around the tower. Racamoni shoved up her glasses and joined in, doing the best she could without falling over her trousers.

Fantastic! Vince loved dancing!

Wahooo!

He started jumping and hopping like mad.

Now the monster was shouting and waving one hand in the air.

What was that noise?

CHUGGA CHUGG CHUGGA.

One of the numbers had started zooming towards them.

CHUGGA CHUGG CHUGGA.

"Keep going!" cried the monster. "We don't want it turning off at the last minute!"

The number was heading straight for them.

As it approached Vince could see it really was like a little number-one-shaped bus. With a single row of number-one-shaped windows rising all the way up it.

COOL.

But – Aaaaagh!

It was getting rather big.

CLOSER.

BIGGER.

CLOSER.

Vince ducked down behind Racamoni, who was whooping and clapping with glee.

What was she so happy about?? They were about to be squashed like tomatoes!!

Daah!

CHG.CHG.CHG.CHG.

Hang on.

The noise had changed.

And he hadn't been squashed.

He peeped round Racamoni.

The Number One was right next to them!

It was!

It had landed as lightly as a feather!!

It was huge!!!

It was as big as a real bus!!!

No, bigger!

And the driver was revving the engine, fiddling with his bright red helmet.

Helmet?!

There was a name printed across the top of it.

"*Moo Shaker…*" read Vince.

Hmm.

Strange.

But the monster was calling him.

"Hop up, and let's hop on!" it giggled. Vince climbed back onto him, and before he knew it, the monster had leapt onto the roof of the bus.

39   Off to a Good Start

A rush of noise met Vince's ears.

The top of the bus was packed with people crammed onto tiny seats.

Some were reading papers, books, magazines. Others were laughing and chattering excitedly.

"Where are you off to?? Oooh Number Eight!...Spendlodes... shopping...lovely!...Number Two? That's next! But it's so fast isn't it! We'll have to be quick to catch that one!!"

Vince's eyes bulged as he took in the scene.

Suddenly somebody grabbed his hand and stamped something onto it.

"OW!" cried Vince. There was a big red "1" on his hand.

"Don't worry," said the monster, its eyes gleaming. "That's your ticket."

"Ready?" it said. "Racamoni, the beach is Number Four. We'll have to do two and three in between. They won't let us on if we haven't covered all the numbers in order."

Vince was about to ask which number Home was, but a bell had begun to ring.

"Oooh...quick!...D'you mind?...Hey! That's my window!...Get off!"

Everyone on the bus had leapt to their feet and started leaning over the sides.

And now the monster was at it!!

Aaaagh!

Vince clung on for dear life as the monster dangled its front paws over the side.

No-o!

Racamoni, who for some reason had tucked her jacket tight into her trousers and rolled her trouser legs up to look like shorts, was now climbing along the monster's neck to get a better view!!

Was she mad!!! He'd have to try and stop her…

DING DING…WOOOOOSH!!

Too late!

At the sound of the second bell the bus had lurched into action and started whizzing back up into the sky.

WO-ah!

As they got higher and higher, passengers began craning their necks as far as they dared to see other buses shooting by.

"There's one!"

Everybody turned to see.

"Ah, no, it's a Number Three! Sorry!"

There was a collective moan.

WOOOSH. WOOOSH.

Vince's head swayed one way and then the next as they rode their crazy ride through the sky.

And then there it was.

"A Two! A Two!"

Down to the left of their bus, Vince could see a bright blue shiny bus zig zagging around. He couldn't see the shape, but it was obviously right, because suddenly everyone jumped.

They did.

Everyone jumped off the bus and began falling towards the Number Two. Some opened parachutes, others umbrellas. Others just flapped their arms and hoped.

As for the monster, he was galloping like a race horse, and shrieking with glee!

Vince wasn't laughing.

AAAAAAAGH!!!

He thought his fingers might break as he held onto the monster's toothy back. His skin was stretched across his face as if he'd been hung out on a washing line to dry. His jacket billowed out behind him like white flapping wings.

AAAAAAAGH!!!

Now he knew why Racamoni had tucked in all her clothes! And she was having a whale of a time! She was pushing back her glasses and whooping as she swung from the monster's neck.

And he was talking all the while.

"Oooh. He's a cheeky one. Weehee! Look! He's seen us! He's skidding off that way! If I turn a bit, we should land on him!!"

Vince looked wildly down.

The monster was right.

They were catching the Number Two.

GALLOP. GALLOP.

Nearer. Nearer.

BUMPF!!!!

The monster had landed.

"Ha! Ha! Hee! Hee!" He and Racamoni did a victory dance across the top of the bus!!!

Even Vince couldn't help smiling as he was jostled around on the monster's back.

He had to admit that was one of the best bus rides he'd ever had in his life.

And other lucky passengers were dropping onto the bus now.

Ooh. Hang on.

What about the ones that missed??

Vince peered over the edge.

Far below he could see their Number One zooming back and forth, catching the unlucky passengers ready for another go.

He nodded.

He liked Skop Hotch! A lot!!!

40 Missed it!

It was very noisy on the Number Two. People were slapping each other on the back, congratulating each other on their successful jumps.

"OOf! Never thought we'd find one!...I know, I can't be late for my meeting! The Number Three had better be easier...Did you see it dive away! I swear it nearly lost me!!...Oooh! Is it stickers today? Thanks Mr HandsUp."

Vince perked up. Stickers? What Stickers?

STICK!

Oh, these stickers!

Someone had plonked a sticker onto his white (well, ish) jacket.

Vince peered down his nose. It was a star. And there were some words...m...no hang on, it's upside down...w...e...l...l...d...well done!

Well done!!

Vince puffed out his chest. It was just like the stickers he had at school.

And in fact, now that he looked around him, the whole bus looked a bit like his school!

Everyone was sitting on benches like the ones in his science lab!

There were pencils all over the floor!

And the walls were lined with shelves packed with books! Vince turned his head to read the spine of one of them.

"H-o-t-c-h-o-l-ogy." He raised his eyebrows. What else? "Add…Adding down made easy…Adding *down*??"

Vince screwed up his nose. What was…?

Oh, hang on, some of the children on the bus were disappearing towards the back.

Were they jumping off??

Vince lowered himself off the monster and wandered over to see.

Ooh.

They *were* jumping.

But they were jumping down a slide which led inside the bus.

Whoosh!

Vince stared at the slide, open mouthed.

Weeeee!

He thought back to his arrival in Oops.

Whizzzz!

So … had his kitchen been a bus all long??!!

And… what was at the end of this slide then??

A chirping voice behind him stopped him in his tracks.

"Don't go any closer Vince. This isn't your Hotch."

It was the monster.

"Anyway, this Hotch is boring. They're all going into lessons!"

Vince's jaw dropped, but there was no time to think, as someone was calling everyone to attention.

"Alright, settle down everyone!" A man carrying a satchel with stickers spilling out of it was standing at the front of the bus, which Vince now realised was a huge blackboard.

He had one finger over his mouth, signalling to everyone to be quiet, and he was holding his other hand high in the air.

The bus fell silent.

When Mr HandsUp was satisfied, he reached into the satchel and drew out a long piece of white chalk.

Turning to the blackboard, he slowly drew a giant tick.

Vince held his breath.

As he lifted the chalk – DING DING!

They were off again! Jerking back and forth in the sky!

Arms and legs dangled over the edge of the bus in anticipation!!

DING! DING!

And there was a Number Three! Straight Away!!

WEEEEEEEEEEEEEEEEEEEE!

This time Vince was really going to enjoy himself.

As the monster jumped, he kicked out his legs and threw back his head.

It was like being shot from a catapult. Vince's jacket was pulled tight round his neck. His legs flew off the monster's back and waved wildly in the rushing air. He was hanging on for dear life.

Daaah! Forgot to tuck in the trousers!

The monster was giving his running commentary as usual.

"Oooh. This is a tough one. It's using reverse as well. I can't keep up with it!!!"

Vince blinked and blinked as he tried to see down below.

The shiny yellow Number Three certainly didn't look like it wanted to be caught.

Passengers were shooting past it, as it ducked and dived. Woo! It even did a somersault!

Vince caught glimpses of the driver grinning from ear to ear in his bright blue helmet as he spun the steering wheel this way and that.

Now the monster was charging through the air, right above the bus.

"I'm going for it!" he cried, as the bus was beneath them.

Vince blinked.

It was getting closer.

BLINK. BLINK.

Oh there it was right there!

BLINK. BLINK.

The monster was lowering his legs for landing.

But...EEEEEK!

With a screeching of brakes, the Number Three had stopped in mid air and started to reverse.

DAAAAAh!

The monster's feet clipped the side of the bus and bounced off again!

No!!!!

They all rolled over and over in the sky from the collision.

AAAAAAAGH!

They were falling, falling. Racamoni and Vince sky dived as the monster fell from beneath them.

Come on. Come on.

Where was the Number Two???

BUMPF.

OUCH!

Oh. There it was.

41   You Cheating Fruit Shop!

"I can't believe it!...I'm going to miss my meeting for sure now!...That's the first time I haven't reached a Number Three you know…"

Vince, Racamoni and the monster sat miserably on the Number Two with the other failed passengers.

Gradually, the bus fell silent.

Vince hunched his shoulders and tried to think.

Racamoni tutted and tried to roll her trousers up a bit higher.

The monster tried to be positive.

"Come on troops," it said encouragingly. "Let's have another go! That was a great roll we did just then! Fantastic!"

Vince nodded. It was a great roll. But he didn't like losing. They'd better get on next time.

And time it was!!

DING. DING.

The noise level rose on the bus again as passengers got ready for another go.

Ding DING.

Vince was getting braver at looking over the edge of the bus.

There seemed to be hundreds of buses whizzing back and forth now.

Seven… Two… there must be a Three somewhere!!!

Suddenly Racamoni began gabbling very fast.

"Dair undi atey! Dair undi atey!" She pointed and waved furiously.

Vince had no idea what she was talking about. Fortunately, nor did the rest of the bus.

But the monster did.

"Oh, you clever girl!" he cried. "You GENIUS!!! You are WASTED in that kitchen, you know. You could do so much better! Get on! Get ON you two!!"

As Racamoni and Vince scrambled up, the monster leapt into space and began shooting downwards. Other passengers jumped uncertainly after him. But where was he going?

And then Vince saw it.

A Number Three bus was cleverly hiding itself right in front of a Number Eight. Their curves matched each other perfectly, and they were racing along together, trying to look inconspicuous. Clothes on rails flapped wildly through the windows of the Number Eight.

"We've got him this time!" squealed the monster. He was galloping towards the Number Three, catching it, catching it. They'd be on in a moment.

BONK!

"OW!!"

They dived away from the bus. The monster had been hit by something.

"That's not fair!" he yelled at the disappearing bus. "You cheating fruit shop! You can't throw apples, it's against the rules!"

They hovered in mid air for a moment, other passengers careering past and landing on the Number Two below.

Vince pushed the hair out of his eyes as the wind dropped. He puffed out his cheeks, resigned to going back to the Number Two once more.

But the monster was still treading air.

Racamoni tried to chivvy him along. "Turnie gin," she said encouragingly.

But the monster seemed to have other ideas.

He was looking around sneakily and muttering to himself.

"If that's the way they want to play, that's fine by me," he said.

Vince began to panic. The Number Two looked pretty full. What if they couldn't get back on???

"Let's go!" he urged.

"Don't worry, we're going!!" shouted the monster, and suddenly leapt in the opposite direction to the Number Two, chasing another bus which had gone shooting past.

It was a Number Four!

"Hey!" yelled Vince as he tried not to fall off. "You can't do that! That's cheating!"

"If they can cheat, so can I!" came the angry response.

Vince swallowed and hung on.

They were catching the Number Four easily. It wasn't expecting them.

Faster. Faster.

Vince gritted his teeth, his legs were taking off again, trousers billowing.

Racamoni jigged up and down excitedly.

With one final stride, the monster leapt on.

42 Racamoni Gets Her Holiday

FFTTT.

FFFTT.

They had landed very softly, in something tickly and grainy.

SAND!

This was the beach alright!

MMMMMM.

What a lovely, sun lotion-y smell!

And – Oooh! Deck chairs!

Vince sighed a relaxed, holiday-mood sigh.

"Sssh!" whispered the monster. "We're in luck, he's asleep."

He pointed to the far corner of the bus, where the conductor was snoring in one of the chairs.

Vince screwed up his nose.

He didn't look very "sunny".

He was well, grey.

Grey swimming trunks, grey sun hat, grey skin.

Racamoni slid down onto the floor. She tidied her jacket and pushed up her glasses. Then with a kiss for the monster and a wave to Vince, she began tiptoeing silently towards the slide.

She climbed into the top.

Ooh. She was a bit big for the hole.

Vince and the monster crept over.

With one giant shove of his paw, the monster pushed her down.

"Weeeeeeee!"

Racamoni's gleeful whoops became quieter and quieter as she raced down the slide.

The monster and Vince listened happily.

But then…

"Very clever," came a voice from behind.

Vince froze.

It was the conductor.

He'd woken up.

And he didn't sound too pleased.

43   The Monster Explodes

"I'll have to fine you of course," said the conductor. He spoke as if he had a peg on his nose. "And you know you'll have to go back onto a Number One and start again."

The monster groaned quietly to itself.

"Jobsworth," he hissed, without looking round. "Didn't recognise him in a swimsuit. What's he doing on this bus? He's normally on a Number Ten."

Vince frowned, confused. He looked round to see Jobsworth scribbling furiously in his notebook and muttering to himself. Now Vince looked more closely, he could see grey globs of sun tan lotion smeared up and down his arms and legs.

The nose peg voice droned on.

"Illegal boarding of a Number Four without the appropriate stamps."

SNAP!

He had leant so hard on his pencil that the lead had broken.

He hurriedly shoved the pencil in a grey, drab beach bag.

"Right…time to call a Number One."

He reached for the badge on his hat, which Vince could now see read "JOBSWORTH", followed by several grey stars. Jobsworth carefully pushed two of the stars and disco music filled the bus.

Despite his rising panic, Vince was very impressed. But he didn't get the chance to see any more, because the monster suddenly pulled him onto his back with a giant swoop of his paw and jumped off the bus!

He did!

AAAAGH!

There they were again, riding through the sky. Oh, Vince had had enough of trying to stay on. He just wanted to go home.

And now he could hear Jobsworth shouting far behind them: "Emergency! Assistance required on bus Number Three point Seven, location corner of Halfway Street and Moonwalk. Fugitives joyriding in direction of Squeezy Lemon Junction."

What???

NEEE NAR NEE NAR.

And what was THAT?!!

Vince swung round.

The glitterball was opening.

AAAAAGH!

From the darkness within it, there emerged…er…nothing.

Vince screwed up his nose, desperately looking (and secretly hoping) for some kind of police bus.

NEEE NAR NEE NAR.

The noise was getting louder, but he couldn't see anything.

How could that be??

"Where is it!?" he yelled to the monster.

"That'll be PCs Burble and Dense!" answered the monster breathlessly. "Look for the flashing blue light. Their bus is invisible, but they haven't worked out how to turn their lights off yet!"

Vince searched the skies wildly.

NEE NAR NEE NAR

"I can see it!" yelled Vince suddenly. Scooting along behind them was a tiny blue flashing light.

"Don't you worry!" said the monster calmly. "I can see what I want too!"

Vince followed the monster's gaze.

Far below he could make out another bus. A Number…Nine.

"Is that it?" yelled Vince. "Is that the way home??"

"Certainly is!" cried the monster. "And we're going to catch it!!!"

He began racing even faster, faster than ever before.

NEEE NAR NEEE NAR

But the police bus was quick too. And it was closing in!!

"Nearly there!" gasped the monster as he bounded onto the Number Nine, knocking over the conductor, who splashed backwards onto a muddy floor.

EEEER!

Vince wasn't very keen on his sludgy home bus!

And – wo-ah! – the monster had tipped Vince off his back, straight into the mud!

SPLATTER!

DAAH!

"No time for worrying about the mess, Vince!" ordered the monster. "Down that slide, now!"

Vince sloshed over to the slide. And stopped.

"But what about you??" he said frantically, as the blue light screeched to a halt alongside them.

The monster's face broke into a huge grin.

"Don't worry about me," he tittered. "They won't know where to start looking!"

And with that…

BANG!!!

The monster exploded into thousands of tiny teeth, which began chattering and scooting around all over the bus, in the sky, in the mud.

TINKLE. TINKLE. TINKLE.

Vince's jaw dropped.

"Monster!"

44   "Hands – Off!"

TINKLE. TINKLE. TINKLE.

Teeth continued to chatter past Vince.

TINKLE.

He stood stock still, his eyes shooting from side to side in their sockets, watching the floating teeth in amazement.

TINKLE.

Dare he catch one? His hands were itching on the ends of his arms…

TINKLE. TINKLE.

He didn't hear the police car screech to a halt beside the bus.

TINKLE.

He didn't hear Burble and Dense boarding the bus.

TINKLE.

He didn't hear them trying to slop their way towards him on the bus.

TINKLE. WINK.

WINK??

Vince shook his head.

Did that floating tooth really just wink at him as it passed by??

"Look out Vince!"

Vince jumped as a voice whispered in his ear.

The tooth was hovering beside him.

"Behind you…"

Vince spun round.

Squelch. Squelch.

Someone or something was coming through the mud!

But he couldn't see anything!

Squelch.

He could sense someone close by.

Where were they?

Squelch. Squelch.

DaaaaH!

Now he saw them!

A pair of hand cuffs seemed to be flying through the air towards him, held by…well, a sort of dot to dot man, legs going like the clappers!

Oooh – he'd never seen that before!

He shook his head. No time to be impressed in Oops.

Think! Think!

PC Dense was nearly upon Vince, and now Vince could make out another dot to dot man who was blocking his entrance to the slide!

Think! Think!

What would he do at home???

Think…RUGBY! Yes!

Vince ran away from the approaching handcuffs and waded towards the slide as fast as he could. He dropped his shoulder and aimed it at the dot to dot policeman blocking his way.

"Doof!" gasped Burble, as Vince knocked him off his feet!

Yes!

But here was Dense approaching with his handcuffs from behind again.

BAFF!

He wasn't expecting Vince's world famous "hand-off" manoeuvre which Vince had perfected on tackles with Dad. Dense was sent sprawling to the ground as Vince's muddy hand thrust into his face.

The two policemen struggled in the slosh, as Vince stood above them, hands on hips, taking a moment to bask in his glory.

He nodded happily and leapt over them into the slide.

He pushed himself off.

WEEEEEEEEEEEEEEE!

He was going home at last!!!!

45   Vince Gets a Smart Kard

SLURP. SQUELCH.

SLURP. SLURP. SQUELCH. SQUELCH.

EEEEER.

Vince had landed.

Landed in something very soft and squidgy.

He blinked around him in the darkness, trying to make something out.

Where was he?

What was he sitting in?

And –

AAAAGH!!!

Something had grabbed him and was roughly pushing his shoulders backwards and forwards.

"OW!" yelped Vince.

"Shorty!" came a lady's voice through the darkness. "Leave him alone!"

Vince smiled as he recognised the voice.

But the pushing got faster.

"Don't worry, Boss," came a breathless voice from behind him. "I've overpowered the intruder! He won't give us any trouble!"

Vince thought he heard a slight groan.

"I-T'-S V-I-N-C-E!" said the lady, slowly, painfully. The pushing stopped. And Vince was tipped unceremoniously forward into something soft and soggy.

Pah!

He spat it from his mouth and peered through the darkness.

Yep, he was back in his garden and…eeeeeer…he was squelching around in his soggy sand pit.

Polly was speaking again.

"Sorry about that. Fantastic job, Invincible Vince," she said, leaning in, and winking at him. "That was a great first bit of *fyxing*."

She frowned suddenly.

"Charmer! Will you be quiet!!!"

Vince turned to see a small tree whispering frantically into its leaves. You could barely see its sunglasses.

It stopped whispering and looked up furtively.

Polly continued.

"As I was saying…Vince, good work. Now…" she reached into her trunk. "We need to find you a new secret sign."

Vince screwed up his nose.

Polly looked at him.

"You know…something that will tell you when you next need to go into Oops."

Vince blinked for a moment, and then opened his mouth to say something, but Polly held up a branch.

"I know what you're going to say," she whispered quickly. "It won't be pink this time. The Boys got you mixed up with a girl doing another job." She rolled her eyes in their direction, and rummaged a bit more.

"Here we are," she said finally.

She held out a gold plastic card to Vince. It looked just like Dad's credit card.

Vince turned it over in his hands. Gold was good. Very good. But he'd actually been hoping for something with wheels.

"It's a Smart Kard," said Polly, putting up a branch once more, smiling. "Yes, yes…it is named after me. Keep it safely hidden, and wait for it to give you a sign." She moved in closer. "In the meantime, you can use it at any bank – your code is 2727, obviously." And she was gone.

Vince blinked at where her face had been in the tree.

Then he blinked down at the Kard.

What did she mean?

He looked around him nervously.

What code?

He shivered.

He needed to get out of the sand pit and into his warm bed.

He jumped out holding the Kard tightly, and began running towards the house.

He ducked as he passed the Boys.

But there was no attack this time.

The sunglasses were gone.

The leaves were still.

He screwed up his nose and charged into the house, his mind racing with his adventure…Lips and chefs and monsters and…Vince stopped.

Monsters.

Monster trucks!

He suddenly knew where Mum's recipe book had got to!!

He'd used it to make a ramp for his trucks that afternoon!

He dived into the kitchen.

Everyone was asleep.

Quickly, he slipped the huge book from his ramp and replaced it on the shelf.

As he climbed the stairs to his room, he stopped suddenly, blinking. He quickly shone his torch onto his pyjamas and looked down at them.

Phew! Helicopter was still there.

He breathed again and carried on climbing. He crept to his secret stash between the bed and the wall and placed the Kard in his treasure box.

He looked at it for a moment…code 2727???

He shook his head, and climbed into bed, yawning a big yawn. "Haaaaah," he sighed contentedly.

But he didn't go to sleep. He stared up at the ceiling, thinking.

What if *FYX/its* weren't supposed to sleep?

What if they had to always be on guard?

What if…?

His eyelids were flickering.

And were there any ghosts in Oops?

Or maybe some massive, fantastic machines that he'd hadn't even seen yet?!

Or maybe…

Zzzzzzzzzzzz.

The End is Only the Beginning

Good.

He's gone to sleep.

And now you know all about Oops and Vince's first mission as a *FYX/it*.

You never know, you could be called up yourself one day. You might want to practise the Oops Jump, just in case.

Because the Sess-Pitts are not the only bad eggs in Oops.

Oh no.

There's plenty more where they came from.

And listen – can you hear that noise?

It's coming from Vince's secret stash.

That's the Smart Kard.

Already jumping around.

There's more trouble looming in Oops.

Rest well, Vince. I think *FYX/it 27* might be in action again pretty soon.